MARK TWAIN

ON THE MOON

Book One: Prospectors!

by

Michael Schulkins

Other books by Michael Schulkins

Beltway

Mother Lode

Sting Suite

Up a Tree: A Jobs and Plunkitt Galactic Adventure

Contact the author at schulkins1@gmail.com
or visit michaelschulkins.com

Book One: Prospectors!

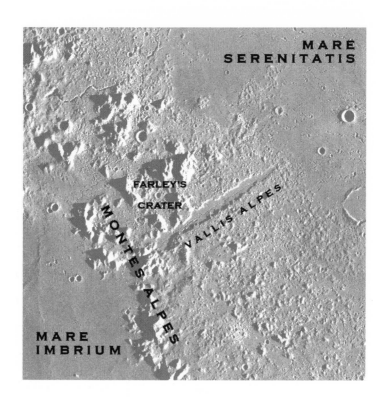

Chapter One

When I was very young, really only a boy, I ran away from home and signed onto a steamboat to see the world, or at least that portion of it between St. Louis and New Orleans. This taste of adventure was so delicious that it ultimately put an end to my tenure on the Earth. It whet my appetite for distant shores— and none is more remote, even in this extravagant age, than the Moon.

My desire for peregrination came to a head through my apprenticeship to a printer, who in order to make ends meet and ruin his reputation, also published a newspaper. While I set its type, I chanced to read this four-sheet wonder—usually upside down and backwards, which made it go down easier. There was not a great deal in it to fire the imagination and wanderlust of a lad recently burst out of his teens, but buried amongst the highly speculative riverboat timetables, stories of steam buggy collisions and the occasional heroic rescue of a kitten stranded on a snag, were tales of the outside world—and the most outside of any of these was of course the Moon.

If only the least spectacular of these stories were true, I reasoned, then all the riches of the heavens, and by far the greatest portion of the adventure available in this life, was to be found there—and it didn't take many of these breathless, hyperbolic accounts to try my patience to its breaking point. There was, a mere two-hundred-and-fifty-thousand miles distant, quite literally an entire new world open for business and available for adventure, and as I read of the mountains of ice ore and caches of gold, silver, and other precious metals being pulled from the planet's vitals every day—without me being there to share in it—I grew restive, then perturbed, and at last feverish with a desire not far removed from lust to see the place for myself, to drink up every drop of trouble and excitement it had to offer, and incidentally to make myself shamefully, ludicrously rich in the process. And remarkably enough, I succeeded in every one of these, although not in any way that I might have imagined while I was busy setting type.

So I stole watermelons out of the fields for my breakfast, ate a rich bowl of Mississippi river water for supper, and saved up my wages until I had enough for the passage. Then with nary a backward glance I lit out for Florida, where the great outer space ships regularly tore themselves free from the Earth's embrace.

These wondrous craft are fueled by seawater, which is ripped apart into its several atoms by voracious resonance engines, and the hydrogen and oxygen thus released are recombined with spectacular violence to produce what is called thrust. This propels each massive vessel along a mile-long set of rails that gradually lifts it into the sky over the Atlantic, traveling at a speed that would make a railroad locomotive at full throttle appear to be standing still. This, as you might imagine, is the exciting part of the trip, although when you actually board the ship you will see none of it, since portholes are not part of the entertainment.

I was sorry to discover that the remainder of the passage is thoroughly uninteresting for the passenger, whenever it is not profoundly unpleasant. He is strapped into a barber's chair, not a foot removed from his fellow voyagers secured to their own barber's chairs on either side, given nothing for company but a small rubber-lined sack (the use for which soon becomes distressingly apparent) and is enthusiastically not permitted to smoke. And he cannot remove himself to the saloon or the texas to smoke and admire the view, because there is no saloon and no texas, and no view for that matter, only the barber's chairs—and no barber either. The saloon, texas, hurricane deck and the entertainments they provide are sorely missed, especially by those accustomed to traveling in steamboats, but, once the horrendous rattling and roaring and oppressive heaviness that comes with escaping the Earth is done, the passenger then misses something much closer to home, namely his own weight, as the gravitational pull he is accustomed to on Earth disappears entirely. This is when the restraining belts come into play, and the ignominious role of the empty sack is revealed, for once gravitation departs all the passengers immediately become seasick (or outer-space-sick, I suppose) and from then on, the atmosphere in the ship strongly resembles the anteroom to Hell. Fortunately, some semblance of weight returns when "thrust" is applied, which occurs at irregular intervals throughout the voyage, presumably because a steady diet of nausea is unfulfilling. Eventually, however, the fun must come to an end, and the passenger finds himself deposited, much the worse for wear, onto the surface of the Moon. Or so he is told anyway, since not a hint of it can be seen. Before he can glimpse even a single crater or craggy escarpment, he is safely buried underground.

Chapter Two

This was how I found myself on the Moon, or in the Moon perhaps, very light on my feet due to the low gravity, and even lighter in the pocketbook, since I'd spent everything I had on securing my passage.

The Moon did offer employment, but not for typesetters or any other job in the printing line. It turned out that there was very little paper to be had, precious few trees to make it from, and none at all to be wasted on newsprint. Nor were there any riverboats to pilot. This reduced my immediate prospects for employment, to be sure, but that did not much disappoint me. I had not come a quarter of a million miles into the void to spend my days setting type. I had come for excitement and adventure, and a chance at riches beyond my wildest dreams.

So I decided to become a miner, despite an entire lack of knowledge, training, or apparent aptitude for the work. This put me right away in the majority thereabouts, since nearly everyone on the Moon, and his dog too if he has one, is a miner, or at least fancies himself one, and that is enough to be accepted into polite society. Of course, there are those who labor behind the scenes, such as farmers, cooks, saloon keepers, smiths, and mechanics, quietly assisting those engaged in the Great Enterprise of looting the planet, but since they are not miners, these unfortunates are held universally in contempt, even by themselves—much like revenue agents, or the fleas on a dog.

I applied for a position, any position, at the offices of Lunar Consolidated Mines, which were not coincidentally underground and hard by the "space port," that being what those in-the-know call the blasted plain where the great ships continually rise and descend, and much to my surprise and delight, I was accepted for work and assigned the job of "picker."

This was in truth a dreadful occupation, but I loved it at first, because the nature of the work allowed, or rather demanded, that I roam about on the bare surface of the Moon in a pressure suit, and do so day after day, in the roasting sun or the freezing night. (There are only the two of these to choose from on the surface of the Moon.) The novelty of this experience was enjoyable, at least until the tedium and discomfort of it took hold. In this I was exceedingly lucky, because there were any number of men—strong, determined, otherwise courageous men; bold, intrepid, lavishly calloused, mulishly stubborn, profoundly stupid men—who could not tolerate the work at all.

The difficulty was not in the task of picking itself, the performance of which is so simple you could train an ape to do it, likely in ten to fifteen minutes—but because the work is done, day after day for hours on end, in a pressure suit—and some men, quite a few men as it happens, cannot tolerate wearing the thing, and once free of its confines after an initial acquaintance, will never deign to step inside one again. The reasons for this shyness are legion, and all of them quite sound. First and foremost, there is the profound and unrelenting sense of confinement, since you are encased in an inflated, lead-lined, canvas sack with a metal bowl over your head, and the only access to the outside world—which will kill you in ten seconds flat in any case—is a radio set, and an eight-inch diameter piece of glass situated an inch from your nose. Then there is the smell, and all of the personal unpleasantness that goes into the production of it. Next there is the extreme heat, and the extreme cold, whichever one of these you draw depending on the time of day. (Day—just the part when the sun is in the sky, mind you—lasts for two weeks straight on the Moon, and has worn out its welcome in a fraction of that time.) There is the nightmarish sensation of asphyxiation that sneaks in when your air supply runs low, to say nothing of the peaceful death that soon follows if you do not replenish it promptly. There is urinating into a tube, without the use of your hands, and there is the consequence of missing it. And last but not least, there is the itching, with no opportunity to relieve oneself by even the tiniest scratch. This brand of suffering comes in two varieties, by the way: one entirely self-inflicted, and the other enhanced through the assistance of fleas. This last complaint may sound trivial, but to the man unable to overcome it, it is the sheerest agony, and more than once in a single Earth day I have seen a man, once again a strong, seemingly stolid man who could lick me in an instant, be decanted from his pressure suit gibbering and screaming for mercy, reduced to near madness by the unrequited urge to scratch every inch of himself raw.

None of the men so afflicted will ever make a miner, not for so much as an afternoon's entertainment—for being a miner absolutely requires that you spend most of your waking hours, and likely some of the unconscious ones, inside such a suit.

For my part, I experienced the same predations and privations as everyone else who put on a pressure suit and strode onto the surface. There was no escaping them. But, for no reason I will ever understand, none of these admittedly unpleasant things bothered me much. I complained about all of them with enthusiasm, to be sure, as that was about all we had for entertainment, but somehow my heart wasn't in it.

The end result of this form of "natural selection," if you will, was that many men were called to be pickers, but few were chosen, and thus the wages were good. The challenge was to stick it out long enough to make it pay.

Now, the kind of mining practiced by Lunar Consolidated Mines is known as strip mining, and a more tedious, indifferent method for wresting value from the surface of the Moon, or the Earth for that matter, has yet to be devised. It consists of gathering up vast quantities of the Lunar surface, thoroughly without regard to its content—the presence of a gold nugget, a picker's abandoned "toothpick," or the desiccated remains of the picker himself for that matter, being considered a bonus—and pulverizing the collected material until its best friend wouldn't know it. Once pulverized, it is sold off for a penny a pound—gold nuggets, toothpicks, and deceased pickers no doubt fetching a slightly better price.

The dredging up of this humble material is done by huge ambulatory machines that operate on the noble principle of Archimedes. (I refer here to the principle of the screw, not the business with the bathtub.) This is considered by everyone, at least everyone in on the joke, to be the most efficient way to handle the chore of removing great stretches of the Lunar surface—the new-fangled principle of the vacuum cleaner being impractical, as the basic ingredient is there in too great a supply. A "scraper" or "pig," as these machines are called, is a large steam-powered tractor a dozen yards high, with a great scoop nearly as wide for a "snout." Inside, behind the snout, are a pair of the celebrated screws, which shove the latest parcel of real estate back and up into a colossal bin, where it waits out the trip on its way to being pulverized. All of this commotion rides along on tractor treads (not wheels, which would raise the pig too high off the ground to do its business) and it is here that we find the picker practicing his trade. You see, as anyone with an ounce of respect for the powers of Beelzebub will expect, the tractor treads are forever running afoul of chunks of the Moon, and it is the task of the picker (in practice, a squad made up of four of them) to dislodge those troublesome chunks with his "toothpick," a six-foot-long aluminum rod. (Everything on the Moon not supplied by the Creator as original equipment is made of aluminum.) Using his toothpick, he must probe the treads and gears in search of the offending rock, or more likely rocks, since they often travel in packs, presumably to improve their chances of bringing down a pig. The picker is also called upon to probe the great screws when they fall prey to a jagged boulder, or a discarded toothpick, or any other unhappy bit of flotsam that is disinclined to be "screwed." On occasion, this requires the picker to crawl up the snout and into the area where the trouble is going on —which might sound like entertainment to some, but then so does grand opera, when heard from a distance.

These huge machines do not drive themselves, but perforce must be operated by mere men—and when I say mere, I mean it. There is something in the work, sitting up in the sky doing next to nothing while people suffering privations and indignities on your behalf scurry about beneath you like bugs on a plate, that attracts the nascent tyrant, or at minimum the nascent horse's ass. I imagine Xerxes would have liked the work, and Nero would have adored it. The operator of a scraper, or "pig jockey," is, in his own mind (if such an organ actually exists), a person of great power and tremendous station, and he treats his attendant pickers accordingly, demonstrating a level of care and affection rivaling that of a feudal lord, or a planter of the Old South before Mister Tesla's genius made them obsolete. His magnanimity toward his dear charges is well known. He will, most of the time, bring his pig to a stop when the pickers begin work, and usually remember to clear them out before starting up again. He provides them with a nearly constant stream of lighthearted verbal encouragement and helpful hints for improving their performance, and when he runs over a picker or two in his haste to return to the "barn" for refreshment, he is very sorry for it, even if he is too shy to say so.

I spent the better part of a year as a picker before I finally got "topped off" and made my escape. I could do so with confidence, because once again I had hoarded my wages in anticipation of it. Some, perhaps most, of the men who worked for Lunar Consolidated Mines, hereafter known as the Company, sent their pay home, expecting to set themselves up in relative splendor once they'd returned to terra firma. If they stuck to places like Natchez, Mobile, or even New Orleans, what they'd saved might last them five years, or even a decade if they were frugal. On the other hand, if they chanced to land in New York, it would all be gone in a week. Many of the men were not cut out for parsimony, however, and rapidly converted their earnings into wine, whiskey, imported Earth delicacies, and other entertainments—or, if they were particularly impatient to be rid of them, gambled them away.

I had a better fate in mind for my wages. My friend Calvin Bemis and I had both saved the majority of our pay, so that, when the time was ripe, we could throw over the picking business and set ourselves up to go prospecting: heading out into the vacuous wastes of the Mare Imbrium, or anywhere else with an equally exotic name, to search for really valuable materials not available to a picker or his pig, such as heavy metals, water ice, and the fabled carbonaceous chondrite. Everyone knew that a man would be set for life if he could find an old meteor or comet head buried inside a crater. And as anyone could see, if he was game enough to don a pressure suit and go out onto the surface, there was an infinity of craters out there just begging to be plundered. The fact that neither Calvin nor I would have recognized carbonaceous chondrite if it had been presented to us at a dinner party wearing a white tie and tails didn't bother us in the least. We would discover the intricacies of the thing later, after we'd got rich, or at least after we'd got started. From what information we could gather, the Company would barely notice if we decided to bolt. There were new men arriving from Florida every week ripe for the picking, if they could stand the work. Plus, for some reason—we chalked it up to bad luck or a lack of gumption—topped-off workers who went out prospecting almost always came back empty-handed, and with a much improved attitude toward the picking business. This didn't bother us either. We knew that Company mining was for suckers and weak-Willies, and other inferior types without the brains and the grit to tackle the real job, and no amount of fatherly advice or low sarcasm from mere pickers and pig jockeys was going to change our minds.

The problem was that somehow we could never get started. Oh, we talked it up plenty. In fact, we talked it up until nobody believed us. We even, I suspect, harbored doubts about each other. But providence respected our bluster, even if we didn't ourselves, and at last dealt us a hand that forced us right out of the game. We had a day "chasing pig" that resigned us then and there to quit. It was, as they liked to say on the Mare Imbrium, "the rock that busted the pick."

Chapter Three

The pig jockey we were assigned on that fateful day was one Sven Moleson, although the pickers preferred to call him Fat Boy, and other monikers that are less printable, but only when he wasn't on the radio. Incidentally, radio, which is thought of by the Earthman as a one-way contrivance used primarily for entertainment, has been greatly improved for its duties on the Moon, and is employed ubiquitously for communication, there being no air available to transport sound in the conventional way. In any case, Sven was what you might call "a piece of work," though I'll concede it's unlikely that the Bard had Sven specifically in mind when he coined the phrase. Although his character, to say nothing of his person, was less than pristine in a variety of ways, it was his disposition that made him particularly unbearable, combining as it did the worst traits of a schoolyard bully and a spoiled Ottoman potentate. To his credit, he sported the body of a heavyweight prize fighter, but alas not one in good repair, since only an amorphous mass of blubber and sinew remained, as if he had been cured whole for a number of years in a keg of beer, and not good beer either. His face was broad, in concert with his girth, his nose was inconsequential at best, and his eyes were black, deeply suspicious, and set so close together as to constitute a conspiracy. For these traits, presumably only his ancestors can be held responsible, but in addition he wore a mustache, for which no one can be blamed but himself. Now, I am fond of mustaches as a rule, and entertain one myself whenever I feel the urge, but I must confess that this specimen—Sven's, not mine—was disreputable enough to cast doubt on the entire species. I'll offer you a tour of the thing if you'll dare it, but first send the children out of the room. Sven's mustache started out at a trot and went along fine as a spring day in the early part of its course, thus lulling the spectator into a false complacency, but then, once it ran short of lip to traverse, it lost all confidence in itself and fell upon hard times. Here it began to droop—first only a little, but then precipitously, like a temperance rider falling off the wagon—and at the same time turned from an acceptable if undistinguished brown color to a pale, uncertain, and sickly yellow, and upon achieving this questionable coloration, unraveled itself into a thicket of disparate and disordered strings, like a knitted scarf that has been left overnight with a kitten. Given Sven's easy-going disposition, a careless remark directed at this sorry appendage could earn a picker a black eye back in the barn, and likely a week of "inside work" on the screws of his pig—yet some men thought the thing so deserving as to be worth the risk. Sven was blockheadedly stubborn and demanding on the one hand, and corrupt and lazy on the other, but this is not to say that no one appreciated him. I heard that his wife and children had worked three shifts a day in a foundry in order to raise the money to send him to the Moon, and I, for one, believe it.

Anyway, on the fateful day, four of us were following Sven's pig—he called it Baby, and his affection for the great pile of scrap was legendary—at a respectful distance, and Baby had nearly a full load of rock and dust on board. If we had been following Company procedure, we would have been out twenty yards or so in front "sounding" for boulders and sinkholes with our trusty toothpicks, but Sven didn't like pickers "sittin' in the road" and "messin' up the scenery" (which was nothing but rocks, of course), and after all he was in charge. Besides, Sven would as soon run you into the ground as look at you—so we were content to walk, or hop and shuffle, as one does on the Moon, twenty or so paces behind.

We were enjoying what I believe was the fiftieth in a series of lectures from Sven on how, "if the Company wasn't such a pack of [self-abusers] they'd know how a top pig jock," such as himself, "needs a trip ta Earth every couple months to get his screws greased proper and, hell, why not, even see his wife and his brats if he could find 'em," when Baby reared up like she'd tried to swallow a campaign promise, and was all of a sudden sitting cockeyed, one set of treads spinning. (I was about to say "spinning in the air" but of course that would be a falsehood.) We guessed right away that the pig had run up onto a large boulder, most of which was hidden underground.

Immediately, Sven started calling over the radio, hollering, "Oh Baby! Baby! Baby!" and later, despondently, "Ohh, now my [private part] is in the screws for sure."

Taking the pig jockey at his word, one of the boys decided that, as he put it, "Fat Boy finally figured where to put 'er to Baby to get his satisfaction," but despite considerable effort, no further evidence for this claim was found.

We watched, standing well back, as Baby teetered on that boulder. She was as top-heavy as a coloratura soprano with that full load inside her, and she swayed ponderously from side to side like a gravid hippopotamus perched on a broken bar stool. It was a splendid show, and we pickers stood and gave it all the admiration it deserved. And for Sven, the worst part was that there was nothing in the world he could do about it. So, with no reasonable course open to him, he did what came naturally and started yelling at us.

"You stupid [persons born out of wedlock], this is all your fault. You should'a been out front pokin' the dirt like yer s'pos' to, not draggin' arse back there yakkin' and screwin' off. You get me an' Baby off this [copulative verb] rock before I have ta come down there and murder ya." Then he switched off his radio, apparently to make us sweat.

Well, we considered his request, and the spirit in which it was offered, and decided we really ought to do something, eventually, once we'd thrown up a tent, had some lunch, and rested up a while. One of the boys, being less burdened with principles, I suppose, than those of us who were inclined to view this situation as an opportunity to get in some loafing, pointed out that the Company might dock our pay if the pig got wrecked. Another spoilsport noted that the longer we waited to do something, the longer we'd have to listen to Fat Boy screaming at us, and this in the end was a hard argument to defeat, as once he'd reactivated his radio, there was no way we could make him turn it off again. The prospect of having Sven holler at us over the radio the whole time seemed to take a good deal of the fun out of loafing.

We could escape the heavy rain of invective, but that would require that we turn off the radios inside our pressure suits, and no one in the party was much inclined to do this, not so much because it was against Company policy, but because to voluntarily plunge oneself into total isolation in the lifeless, vacuous, forlorn emptiness of the Moon, miles from what passed, albeit with exceedingly low marks, for civilization, was not to anyone's liking. We could only hope that Sven would choose to keep his radio off.

Now we could have, and in retrospect should have, called in to the barn for help, but two things stopped us. The first was that we were a considerable distance out, and the barn was well over the horizon. This admittedly is not all that far on the Moon, but still someone would have to walk back some part of that distance in order to call in, since radio, as you may or may not know, only works under conditions known as "line of sight." This means that you have to be able to see the fellow, or the pig barn, you wish to converse with, even if just barely. This was especially true when one was forced to use the worn-out sort of radio installed in most Company pressure suits, these generally being sad collections of cracked and fraying wires whose vacuum tubes and condensers were so ancient they may have been left over from the radio set on Noah's ark. The second and perhaps more important reason was that the Company frowned upon a crew of pickers that failed to get their pig out of trouble, no matter how badly trapped it was, to the point that they would indeed dock your pay. True, you might not notice the shortage at first, but you'd be in for a rude awakening one day when you reached into your overalls to pay for a beer and found nothing but Moon dust there.

Thus, over the fading objections of the loafing contingent (which was me), it was determined that something ought to be done. The problem was that none of us seemed to have much of an idea about what that something ought to be. Nevertheless, we eased back up to the pig to have a better look, staying well to the starboard side, since she was listing rather badly to port. With some reluctance, I waved to Sven in his eyrie to switch on Baby's radio, and when he did, told him to stop the treads, and incidentally to pipe down while we looked her over. To his credit, he did as he was asked.

So, having examined all other options and found them wanting, we decided to take an honest look at the situation and see if there was anything we could do. The boulder was huge, so huge that a hundred men, or even one armed with a steam shovel, could not have dug it out, and Baby was sitting directly on top, rolling around on the underside of her screw housing. Then one of the men, Dave Bonner I think his name was, had an idea. If we could tip her over just a bit more to the left, he said, we might get her left tread into the dirt. Then Sven could give her the steam and she might spin around and come off the rock and no harm done. This sounded to the boys like a good plan, its best feature of course being that it didn't require much work.

But Calvin Bemis pointed out that, with the full load she had on, she was more likely than not going to pitch over on her side when Fat Boy engaged the treads. This did seem likely upon full consideration, but the boys hated to give up on a perfectly good plan over so slight a flaw in the theory, so I thought on it a bit and came up with a suggestion that might save it. We'd get Sven to dump the load first, so she wouldn't be so top-heavy. I hailed the pig jockey and asked him what he thought of the plan, but astonishingly, he had not been paying attention, and I had to explain it all again. When I got around to the part about dumping the load, he balked.

"Not a chance, Clemens," he said, "it'll take another six hours to load 'er up again. You chiselin' [persons born out of wedlock again] just wanna collect some overtime." If overtime pay ever existed on the Moon, I never witnessed it. "I'm not bustin' my hump for no pickers. Just do 'er. Baby can make it without a dump."

We tried to bring him around to our way of thinking, but he wouldn't budge. I believe I've mentioned that he was stubborn. So, since it would be his considerable backside that hit the deck if she went over, not any of ours, we agreed to go ahead with the plan without dumping the load. We tipped her until the left treads were touching the ground, and, once the steam was up, Sven engaged the treads. The treads bit into the surface and she started to turn as advertised, but as she came off the top of that rock, the left tread dug into the ground, forcing her snout down into the dust. By the time it had finished, the snout had buried itself all the way up to the screws.

The spinning tread was spitting out a fountain of dust and gravel as it dug itself in, and for my sins I caught a chunk of rock square in the faceplate. The sun shield, a thick slice of smoked glass which is secured over the actual faceplate of one's helmet to ameliorate the effect of the blistering Lunar sunlight, cracked at the blow. I abruptly found myself looking through a spiderweb of fractured glass. Still, far better that the sun shield sacrifice itself than the faceplate, I thought, since the latter was responsible for keeping in all the air. I found, after an anxious check of a gauge, that I wasn't losing pressure. This was a calamity for me to be sure, but not the fatal one it might have been during Lunar night, when I wouldn't have had the sun shield to save me. When compared to the fate of Baby herself, it is reasonable, if not particularly satisfying, to say that I got off light.

The pig was indeed a sorry sight. Her great snout was now thrust deep into the ground. The left tread was mostly buried, and her rear was raised ponderously into the air like a—but alas, the simile that expresses it best is too unkind—and she was still carrying that full load, and listing a solid thirty degrees to port. Naturally, Sven was screaming at such a pitch I thought he was going to bust a gut.

Any sane man would have thrown in his hand at that point and called the barn, but Sven wouldn't hear of it. He threatened to get the Company to, as he put it, "dock yer pay 'til ya starve if anybody tries to go over the hill." Instead he wanted us to dig out the snout and the treads and prop them up with rocks until he could drive the pig out under her own steam. The boys considered this a poor plan upon hearing it, and I was compelled to agree. First of all, they reckoned, the physics of the scheme was questionable (which was probably true, although you couldn't have proven it by me, as I had had limited exposure to that formidable subject at that point in my life and could not have told you the difference between the law of gravitation and a sawhorse, if indeed there is one). In addition to that, and far more destructive in my opinion, was the fact that it promised to involve more honest work than we would customarily do in a month, and that was a flaw not to be casually overlooked. It did have a saving grace though, in that it was clearly impossible.

I suspected we would have a better chance of thrusting our shovels into the Moon dust and striking oil, or French champagne, than we did of digging out that pig before our air ran out, we collapsed from exhaustion, or both. This might appear to be a major flaw in the scheme, as these things are measured, but that is because you are not a pig jockey—for which incidentally you should be grateful until the end of your days. But since Sven's plan was impossible, we felt we could practice at it for an hour or so without doing any more damage to the pig, in fact without accomplishing anything whatever, and by that time Fat Boy, who was not attached to that handle without cause—well, his capacious gut would soon begin to rumble, and his considerable rear section would get sore from sitting up there in his emergency suit at a thirty-degree tilt, and he would eventually give in and send one of us over the horizon to call the barn.

So we retrieved the shovels out of Baby's tool locker and started to pretend to dig her out. We pitched the dust and gravel under the right tread and piled any rocks we came across where Sven could see them. It had sounded like a decent enough way to spend an hour, but before even half of that time had passed, and all the boys had replaced at least one air cylinder, I could tell that just keeping up a good show was likely to kill us.

Doing this kind of work in a pressure suit, in what is paradoxically known as hard vacuum, exposed to the full undiluted violence of the Sun, is so unpleasant as to be indescribable. Nevertheless, I shall try. I once witnessed the strange spectacle of a turkey, a fine twenty-pound bird too, being roasted inside a bag. To its credit, the turkey emerged delightfully moist and tender, as it was cooked entirely in its own juices. In our situation the method was very much the same, and the results identical, only the smell was not so pleasant by half. But then the turkey had a better time of it, since it had the advantage of already being dead. And in addition, if you will recall, I was forced to stare ceaselessly at a fractured glass spiderweb sitting where my sun shield used to be. I could conceivably have removed what was left of the sun shield, but I knew if I did my face would soon peel off, and by the time we got back to the barn I'd be as blind as a worm.

By the time we had been at this fruitless work an hour, it became obvious that Sven was holding up far better than we were. After all, all he had to do was sit up there in the cab and yell at us. And he did that every day, all day long, for a living. We simply couldn't compete. So soon we were in the market for yet another plan. And, wouldn't you know it, there came Dave Bonner to the rescue, once again. Now you may question the wisdom of taking the advice of a serial rescuer, as his repeated efforts only serve to highlight his repeated failures, but this wisdom eluded me at the time.

"First," he said, "we put some flat rocks behind the treads." Remarkably, we had actually uncovered a few of those. "Then," he continued, "Fat—uh, Sven runs the pig's engine in reverse and backs her out of the dust."

"Well," said one of the boys, perhaps it was Bemis, "what about old Mount Everest back there?" referring to the boulder. "Won't it be in the way?"

"Not," said Bonner, the serial rescuer, "if he backs over it with one of the treads. That'll just provide more traction."

Well, this plan was even worse than Sven's, but the boys loved it. The astute reader will notice that it didn't involve much work. I think the boys noticed that too. The hidden pitfall in this new scheme, as if it needed one, lay in the fact that the screws and the treads of a pig are directly linked. If the treads are run in reverse the screws will run in reverse as well, and they're simply not designed to work that way, especially with a full load of Moon dust behind them. I'm certain at least one of us knew that, or should have, but nobody said a thing. Sven was desperate enough by then to try it, and I, half blinded by the ruined sun shield and plenty tender and juicy by then, having baked in my suit, no longer cared, so we went ahead. Or rather, backwards, we hoped.

The treads began running in reverse, and the pig actually started moving rearwards for a few seconds, but then the gears somewhere in her insides locked up and Baby stopped cold. On their radios, the boys worked up a sound like the crowd makes when a ballplayer sends one to the fences and has it caught before it sails over. A round of half-hearted cussing followed, but once that brief squall had passed, no one said a thing.

Then after a minute Sven piped up with, "Damn, she was comin', boys, she was comin' out 'til the [copulating] screws jammed. One a you men crawl up there an' see what's got her stuck."

I was stupid enough to say, "But Fat—but Sven, her snout's chock-full of dust. There's no chance we could get up there."

And Sven said, "Thanks for volunteerin', Clemens. Get yer arse in there. And take your pal Bemis with you."

Calvin and I just looked at each other, not that I could see him of course. Then we looked around for help, but no one was throwing out any life preservers. The other two pickers, including Bonner the serial rescuer, weren't saying a word. All of a sudden there was the worst outbreak of gauge-checking, and sun shield-cleaning, and just plain staring off into space that I'd ever seen. Neither of them wanted to be tagged to go with us.

So, not knowing what else to do, we did as he'd said. Bemis grabbed a shovel and we worked our way around to the snout. We dug out a hole big enough for me to get into, and I got down on my knees and started up, scooping out dust as I went. The going was extremely slow. Each time I dug in a few feet a new collection of rocks and dust would slide down the snout and bury me. The light from my helmet lamp refracting through the fracture in my sun shield made it impossible to see anything, though that wasn't really a problem since there was absolutely nothing to see.

I had nearly forgotten which way I was going when I heard a *bong* on top of my helmet and realized I'd found the screws.

"Calvin, I've got to the screws," I said.

"Good," he said, "I was getting kind of tired of you kicking me in the head."

"Feels good when it stops though, huh?"

"Get on with it, Sam."

I started to work my way up one of the screws. They were just wide enough for a man in a pressure suit to shinny up—if they weren't filled with dirt, which they were. So there was more digging. After about two turns of the screw, I came to a rock that I couldn't budge. It was wedged between the screw itself and the housing. That had to be the rock that had put me there.

I called out to Sven and told him as much. "I think I've found the problem, but I can't budge the rock. And even if I could, it's too big to get it past me," I added.

"Good!" Sven yelled. "Clemens, you have my permission to live."

But then, when I needed it least, Sven hatched an idea. After two hours of stubborn refusals, he decided to dump the load. Only God knows why, so to speak, but the results were so bad that only the Devil could have signed off on it. As the pig's great hopper emptied out, the dirt shifted, the rock that was jamming the screws popped loose, landing on my head as neat as you please, and to my horror the screws started to turn! Sven should have taken the engine out of gear entirely when the screws seized up, but instead had missed his mark and set it to forward again. So Bemis and I rode up the screws, popped out the back of the pig, dropped some thirty feet onto a pile of rocks, and were promptly buried under several tons of dust.

When they finally dug us out we decided we had had just about enough of picking. We figured that prospecting couldn't be anywhere near as frustrating and dangerous as chasing a pig. We were dead wrong about that, of course. The only other good thing that came out of this disaster was that Sven caught the blame for the whole incident and was busted to picker for six months. The opportunity to watch Fat Boy hopping along chasing a pig was almost enough to get us to stay, but we'd promised ourselves we'd go prospecting, so we reluctantly passed it up.

Chapter Four

Oh, what a magnificent thing, to be a prospector!

Bemis and I were so pleased to be embarking at last upon the Great Adventure that we were the very picture of self-satisfaction and supercilious magnanimity. We had not been off the Company payroll for a full day—a paltry Earth day too, not the two-week-long marathon that is the Lunar day—and our sentiments had already begun to mellow toward those quaint old days at the Company mine. We felt only pity for the lowly pickers we had roundly condemned just the day before. From our lofty perch even the hated pig jockeys were worthy of no more than a benign and detached contempt, for we were prospectors. By God, we were high on ourselves. And woe be to anyone foolish enough to cross our path, for they were bound to hear about it. They'd hear about it until they were as full of it as we were.

We had planned our first steps for months, planned them nearly to death, in the obsessive, meticulous, harebrained way that only a man who knows full well his plans will never be realized can do. A prisoner etching routes of escape onto his cell walls is an example of this; a homely gal well past her expiration date looking into wedding gowns would be another.

As a first step we intended to travel to a real mining town. Fortunately there was just such a town nearby, less than a dozen miles to the north. Pickers and other mine workers made occasional visits there in order to unburden themselves of their wages. As Bemis and I had hoarded our gold against this very day, we were entirely innocent of its charms, but this was about to change. The town was called Lucky Strike, and if you think its name somewhat too good to be true then you are correct. If you call a plow horse Greased Lightning in hopes that it will convince him to run, it is comforting to reflect that even if the name does not convince the horse, it may yet convince unwary bystanders that the nag must be a flier. If visitors wished to believe Lucky Strike owed its continued existence and relative prosperity to the questionable success of its prospectors, as opposed to the undoubted success of its saloon keepers, restauranteurs, gaming impresarios, and purveyors of horizontal entertainment, they were most welcome to do so, because it was good for business. Bemis and I were so high on ourselves and the Great Adventure that we were well beyond the reach of reason, and we thought the name grand.

Once there, we would lay out a portion of the gold we had saved for the purchase of equipment and supplies. This money was called a "grub stake" according to Bemis, who had read a sack-full of western stories by Brett Harte and other pathological liars, and thereby fancied himself something of an expert.

Before we could dispose of our grub stake, however, we had to negotiate the dozen or so miles of hard vacuum, as some call it—and trust me, it is indeed hard—between the Company's underground beehive and Lucky Strike. If we were still on Earth, this would have been nothing, a matter of an afternoon stroll in the sunshine, a pleasant two-hour ride atop a horse, or even less time in a hired steam buggy, but this was not the Earth, and a stroll in the sunshine would be the death of us in our present condition, because once we had quit the Company, we were obliged to turn in our Company-issued pressure suits.

This is no small thing, believe me. The truth is, there is no more sorry and forlorn an individual in all Creation than a citizen of the Moon without his pressure suit. A cowboy who lacks horse, bridle, saddle, bedroll, chaps, spurs, six-gun, and his ten-gallon hat is a potentate by comparison. The cowpoke may not be much use at his profession under such circumstances, but unless he mislaid his possessions in a tornado, or relinquished them as a prelude to swinging from the end of a rope, he is likely to survive the loss. This is not so for a resident of the Moon. Without his pressure suit he is as good as dead, and possibly worse.

Now it happens that the Company will sell a topped-off picker, or anyone else who is foolish enough to inquire, a used—and when I say used, believe me I mean it—a used pressure suit at a reasonable price, reasonable for the Company that is, but a polite form of robbery by anyone else's reckoning. And of course the articles in question were Company suits. As you might imagine, Bemis and I were well acquainted with these fellows, and knew them for the low shiftless unreliable breed they were.

Fortunately, there was a way for us to get to Lucky Strike that didn't require a pressure suit. We were obliged to wait another day—a day loaded full to the gunwales with agonized anticipation, I assure you— but if we did we could ride the "bus." It was *the* bus as opposed to *a* bus because like the Moon itself, there was only one, but that one was enough. The bus was a conveyance that ran two or three times a week between Lunar Consolidated and Lucky Strike, taking away mine workers whose pockets were heavy with gold and returning them to the Company a day or two later as light as a feather. If it ever ventured into more interesting territories, I am unaware of it. The bus was a refitted pig with the screws and other machinery removed. The resulting empty space was pressurized, which was essential for our purposes because we had no suits, and was fitted with long, battered aluminum benches to accommodate passengers.

As I've noted, the purpose of the bus was to transport gold from the Company to Lucky Strike using mine workers as handy containers, but there were sometimes other sorts of passengers, such as the occasional group of excursionists come up from Earth to see the sights, if they could find any. And on that particular day we were lucky enough to have several of these worthies aboard. Bemis immediately sensed that they might be ripe for our prospector line and struck up a conversation with the most likely, and not incidentally the most comely, of the excursionists, a young woman from of all places, San Francisco.

"Yes, ma'am," said Bemis, "I'm a miner, sure's yer born. Fact is—Miss Yamamoto is it?—fact is, Miss Yamamoto, my partner Sam here and me, we're not just your plain, everyday, off'a the shelf-type strip miners. No, ma'am, we're prospectors. Which are something like aristocrats, as your miners go. We're real independent, ya see, and tough as the steel tip on a drill head. And we expect to be mighty rich almost any day now."

I could only assume that Calvin had spent some considerable time working up this patter and I didn't want to offend his pride by laughing out loud. I more or less succeeded, but it wasn't easy, and staying silent after hearing about us being mining aristocrats cost me dearly. If he had gone on much longer I fear I would have been obliged to stop the bus and dump my load of pent-up laughter or else explode.

Miss Yamamoto asked about the Company mine, which they had just toured.

"Sure, I used to be a pig jock'," claimed Bemis, falsely, screwing up his face like he'd caught a breeze from the waste treatment plant, "but that ain't a fit job for a man with the real stuff. Prospecting, now that's the genuine article. Nothing less will do for a real man." Miss Y stared at Bemis impassively. "Or a real woman, of course," he concluded. He had squeezed that last part in just under the wire by my reckoning, but he had got it in, and was duly rewarded for it. Miss Yamamoto smiled and blushed just a pinch, and Bemis nearly died and went to Heaven on the spot. And he deserved to, in my opinion.

I had some trouble unhitching Calvin Bemis from Miss Yamamoto when the bus pulled into Lucky Strike, but once she'd asked him why bonafide prospectors such as ourselves didn't have our own pressure suits, and he had failed to invent a whopper in time to escape, most of the fight went out of him, and he soon stuck up his hands and came quietly. I tried to console him by asserting that a prospector couldn't rightly be seen in the company of excursionists. We had to keep up a certain standard, I insisted, seeing as we were aristocrats and all. The irony may have stung a bit as it went in, but the drug took rapid effect, and soon he was back to normal.

Like nearly all towns or facilities on the Moon that are meant to house human beings, or anything else still on the sunny side of the grave, Lucky Strike was built almost entirely below ground. This may be a calamity for the trade in scenic postcards, but there are good reasons for it. It is much easier to keep the air in, for one thing, and it keeps the sunshine, or solar radiation as the scientists like to call it, out. We are told at an early age, and countless times thereafter by innumerable busybodies, that too much of a good thing will prove to be bad for us, and I confess that this is sometimes true. For example, I believe that an overindulgence in temperance will nearly always bring one low, although this may not be what the drummers for this platitude had in mind. Still I will concede that an overabundance of certain items does sometimes produce the reputed effect. I am thinking specifically here of honeybees, small children, literary critics, and congressmen, but then you may have your own list. And so it is with the Sun, or at least his effluvia, especially when that mighty furnace develops a case of dyspepsia and vomits up a solar flare, which I am assured he occasionally does. When this happens the only real remedy is to bury oneself in the ground like a gopher, and wait there until the old boy's digestion improves. So for this reason, and others too numerous to mention, Lucky Strike was situated underground.

Once the garage where the bus was parked had been refilled with air, we disembarked and were directed to a large pressure hatch which, we saw as it opened, led directly onto the main street of Lucky Strike. It was here we discovered that, before we could enter into this promised land, we would be obliged to lay out a portion of our gold for the mere privilege of drawing breath, because Lucky Strike had an air tax. The collection of this tax was administered by a brusque business-like fellow holding a pencil and a receipt book, and secured by the presence of several surly-looking men loafing nearby who seemed to take an abiding interest in polishing their six-guns.

I soon discovered that this air tax operated on a sliding scale, allowing one to discount his air consumption by paying in advance if he chose. Lucky Strike's air cost a man a dollar a day, in gold, if he bought a single day's allotment, but if he had reasonable confidence in his ability to stay alive and available for regular breathing for more than a single day, he could purchase four days for three dollars, or, if he dared hope to live so long, he could have an entire week's breathing for five. Of course if he managed to get himself murdered or dispatched in some other manner short of this time, then the remainder of his outlay would go to waste, so some prudence was called for. I found this business of the sliding scale intriguing and determined to explore it further. I inquired as to what the discount would be if a man purchased an entire year's worth of air in one go. If purchasing this huge allotment saw the price fall to let us say a penny a day, one could breathe all year for three dollars and sixty-five cents (unless it was a leap year) and this would result in quite a considerable savings over the standard rate. Unfortunately, my proposal, as innocent as it was, aroused the interest of the men polishing their pistols, and not in a good way, so I abandoned what I thought was a generous offer and purchased a mere two day's supply at the full rate.

I was understandably disappointed at the failure of my negotiations, but the true rude awakening in this encounter had still to occur. It came when it was made clear to me that the air I had purchased—and at the top rate, I remind you—was not to be given over to me in a steel cylinder or other container that I could carry with me and draw upon as I saw fit, but that I was expected, after paying a premium for the privilege, to breathe the air that was already in circulation. This was used air, previously owned air if you will, and quite extensively pre-owned at that, if its prevailing odor was to be believed, and to my way of thinking this wasn't right. It offended my sensibilities, and what is worse, it offended my pocketbook. I had paid handsomely for the virgin article, I believed, and asserted that I should get it. However, the gentlemen with their gleaming six-guns saw the matter differently, and I had thereafter to content myself with breathing the pre-owned air.

Once we had finished running this gauntlet we were released into Lucky Strike itself, most of which was contained in a single street. This thoroughfare consisted of a rough-hewn, dimly-lit tunnel between five and six yards wide, lined on both sides entirely with saloons. Well, not entirely, but every one that wasn't a saloon was certainly doing its best to blend in. You had to look mighty closely to see the brothels and gambling halls, but they were there. The tunnel that was the main street did not run straight, but instead had a dogleg in it about every three saloons or so, and thus there was a surprise in store around every bend, generally in the form of another saloon. A joyful noise of sorts poured from the entrance to one and all of these establishments. Shouting, laughter, lively disjointed music, and a general happy unfocused mayhem spilled out into the street, forming a river of intoxicating sound that, despite our valiant efforts to resist it, soon swept us away, and we found ourselves following a clutch of men as they strode into one of the saloons.

The place we had chosen, or been led into like a pair of sheep if you must be technical, was called The Eskimo, for no particular reason that I could discern. Bemis speculated that since eskimos were known to reside in the neighborhood of large quantities of ice, and ice was known to be mined on the Moon, a connection could be established along those lines. I thought this something of a stretch, but there was a luxurious polar bear hide nailed to the rock wall behind the bar, its head still attached, eyes shining, mouth agape, and teeth bared. That was a good enough explanation for me. I was content.

Bemis and I worked our way over to the bar for a better view of that polar bear skin, and soon found ourselves occupying a pair of vacant stools. The bar rail was upholstered along its outer edge in what I took to be polar bear fur, with a set of claws sewn in every couple of yards to enhance the effect. We ordered beer on tap and surveyed the crowd. We recognized a disappointingly large number of men we knew from our days with the Company, pickers and pig jockeys and waste plant workers and the like. We ignored them as best we could, being keenly conscious of our new, elevated station. They were equally aware of our magnificence apparently, for they were pleased to ignore us right back. But looking past the pig drivers and such, we spotted other men whom we took to be prospectors. We knew they were prospectors because they weren't wearing Company overalls, and because once we had been accepted into their society by the trick of buying them a round of beers, they told us so. Naturally, we told everyone within range what a pair of blazing hot prospectors we were, and in order to reinforce the proposition, bought additional liquor for anyone who made the slightest pretense of believing us.

Then, at some time during my fifth or sixth drink, Bemis, who had wandered away some time back, presumably on a mission to unship his beer, returned to the bar with a certain look in his eyes. I was not unduly alarmed by this, as his look was akin to the one he got when he thought he had attracted the attentions of a member of the opposite sex, in a manner that did not reek of disdain. In this, as it turned out, I was mistaken, but I don't think I can really be blamed for the error, as Calvin wore the expression only rarely, and was invariably mistaken in it.

He leant close to my ear and whispered, "Sam ol' pal, I got somebody I want you to talk to you—I mean to say, somebody I want you to talk to."

"So she's got a friend, does she?" I said. "It's mighty nice of you to think of me, but I prefer to cut them out of the herd for myself." I was feeling the effects of those five or six drinks by then. "Thanks anyway but—"

"No, no, Sam," he said with an air of drunken reproof, "this is business. Big business, if I'm any judge of what's what."

I puzzled over this for a moment, then gave up on it and said, "Very well, Calvin, lead on. But I plan on keeping both hands on my wallet. And I'm taking along a beer." The difficulty of accomplishing this with only two hands is obvious to the sober, whose ranks no longer included myself, but since it was only a metaphor, I managed it all right.

He led me into the rear of the saloon, where there were a number of private tables being served by a barmaid wearing nothing but a scrap of polar bear fur. Staring, I felt a pang of pity for her. That measly bit of fur wouldn't have kept a penguin warm in Florida if he was marching in a Fourth of July parade. I called to Bemis to hold up for a minute while I stuffed my eyeballs back into their sockets.

To see Calvin Bemis walk past such an apparition without a glance was disturbing. He spied me setting my eyeballs back into place and said, "Not now, Sam, we got business to talk. This i'n't the time." Bemis never talked like that, not about women, and especially not about women like that barmaid, with whom he hadn't a Hottentot's chance in Hell of success, for that was the kind of girl he liked best. I was tempted to ask this stranger who he was, and inquire as to what he had done with the genuine Bemis, but I decided against it, as this new Bemis stood some chance of being an improvement over the original.

We took chairs at a small table, at which one man was already seated. The lighting was poor (as it often is in barrooms) and thus I couldn't be sure, but to me he appeared at least one hundred and twenty years old. But then perhaps not. Like I said, the lighting was poor. He may have been no more than a hundred and ten. This man had no hair on his head to speak of and, as a result of the way in which he drank his beer, I concluded that he also had no teeth to speak with. His skin bore a marked resemblance to that of a turkey, a plucked turkey, in that it was astonishingly wrinkled, was far too roomy for its occupant, and was mottled and stained to the point of being piebald. On his turkey's skin there grew also quite a number of warts and moles, enough warts in my opinion to outfit a sizable regiment of toads. And it's a good thing he had them too, the moles that is, since all the hairs he had left to him were situated there. Now as a rule I don't hold these sorts of things against a man, but there are limits, and this bird had gone beyond the pale.

Bemis turned to me and said, as proud as if he were introducing me to his own father, "Sam, this is Farley. Farley O'Toole. He's a prospector, like us."

About then there was a sound like a pig's screws seizing up on a load of gravel. I looked about me in some concern, but it turned out it was only this fellow Farley speaking to me. "Son," he said, "I been keepin' an eye on you two boys ever since you come in, and you look pretty sound to me. Yep, pretty sound, if I'm any judge, which you kin believe me I is. I know you're in town to set up for a big prospectin' jag, and I think maybe I kin he'p you out. If'n you'll he'p me too, that is."

I said, "Sorry, pop. I don't think we're prepared to take on any partners just yet." This poor old fellow couldn't climb an anthill, I suspected, even in the weak one-sixth gravity of the Moon.

"Naw," he said, "I'm gettin' too old to go diggin' myself. I can't use it no more. That's why I wanna give it to you boys."

"That's what I was trying to tell you, Sam," Bemis said.

"Tell me what?" I said, scratching my head. "Give us what?" This conversation was proving difficult to follow for a man in my impaired condition. "What are the two of you talking about?"

"The map!" they said together.

I wished with all my heart then that I had followed the barmaid.

Chapter Five

"Calvin, I should have guessed you'd come up with something like this. Why can't you stick to chasing women? You never manage to catch any of those." In my drunken wisdom, I was winding up to offer him a piece of my mind.

"Sam—" he began, but immediately I raised a hand and brought him to a halt.

Then I carved off a generous slice of the organ in question and launched it smartly in his direction. "This is just grand," I said, "absolutely brilliant. Let me see if I can summarize for us—and also for posterity, for surely the pedigree of the scheme is so ancient that it's only fit for a museum, if not a mausoleum. Allow me to see if I can encompass the full glorious idiocy of the project before it's too late, while it is still lying in wait, or yet safely mewling in the crib." Having thus prepared the ground, I proceeded to lay out the allegations. "Farley here, whom neither of us knows from the pig driver's cat, is going to, out of the boundless generosity of his somehow still beating heart, sell to us The Map, the sole, singular, and no doubt quite secret map to the

Lost Dutchman Mine, or some other hole in the ground of equal repute. And for the miraculous appearance of this wonder, we are supposed to well-nigh burst at the seams with gratitude. And now for the best part, the indispensable culmination of this epic foolishness, it will only cost us—what?—a thousand dollars, apiece, I'll wager, for the privilege of its receipt." I paused then to stare defiantly, roughly in the direction of Bemis. "May God strike me dead on the spot—" I swore, invoking an oath that is best entertained only when one's confidence is more than usually firm. This is particularly true on the Moon, where the Good Lord has so many convenient tools at hand for completing the job. "May He strike me dead if I don't have the full essence of it right there, in all its naked glory, and I dare you to tell me I don't." I turned on Farley O'Toole then, and in a tone still hot but a degree or two less scalding than I'd directed at Bemis, said, "I'm sorry, old-timer, but even I am not stupid enough, or drunk enough yet, to fall for this one." Fortunately for the health of this tale, if not for my own well-being, I had more liquor to consume. "Calvin's plenty foolish enough, I'll grant you that, but then he knows I'll kill him if he tries it. Don't you, Cal?"

"Now, Sam, you're not being fair to old Farley here. He doesn't want any two thousand dollars for it.

Not even half that. Hell, he's letting it go for next to nothing." What Bemis left unsaid of course was that I was otherwise correct in all particulars. And thus it appeared that God would have to postpone my demise for another day, at least on this account.

As the flaming dissertation above so very well illustrates, I was as bloated with righteous indignation as I was with whiskey and beer. But, in search of relief from this inflated condition, I had thrown the steam-cock wide open, and thus had largely blown myself out—either that, or I had hurled at Bemis such a sizable portion of my brains that there was nothing left. In any case, I looked once again at my friend, my partner in future glory, and upon seeing his excitement and white-hot eagerness to head right out and strike it rich in one ferocious godawful hurry, I suddenly felt I was looking at myself—albeit a few inches shorter, quite a bit darker of complexion, and sporting a much inferior mustache, but nonetheless a reasonably accurate reflection of myself—and my anger melted away. Still, its dissolution left a small but stony pit of skepticism behind.

I downed the remainder of the beer in my glass, sighed dramatically, and said, "All right, Calvin, at least let him deliver the pitch himself. Or have you decided to give me the brush and take up with Farley here instead?" This last was ill-considered, a low blow in fact, and I freely confess it. I reproduce the remark here to demonstrate my fidelity to the truth—which I may have to trot out later in this narrative, when evidence of my veracity is in short supply.

"Aw now, Sam," Calvin said with distressing sincerity, "Don't say that. You're not thinking straight. We're partners, you and me. Partners through thick and thin. You know that." And I did. "But what do you say we take a look at it? What harm could that do?"

"Well fine then," I said, after a moment's consideration. I was no longer indignant, just disgusted—less disgusted with Bemis and increasingly disgusted with myself. Not so much for laying into Bemis, who roundly deserved it, but because despite my exertions I could feel the sand slipping away beneath my feet as I allowed myself to be drawn into this shamefully transparent scheme. I added, "It doesn't cost anything to look, does it, Mister O'Toole?"

Hearing this, the old man began to work over the contents of a large sack he carried, and after a minute's fishing came up with a long tube of paper, which naturally was The Map. He spread it out on the table and we put our glasses on the corners to keep it from curling up. I must confess I found that map to be pretty rough going compared to my usual literature, and it took me a few minutes of staring dumbly at the thing to understand it. To begin with, it contained many millions of contour lines. I had seen such lines before and knew something—but not overly much—of their ways. Follow them on any map that is legitimate, and assuming they are in the mood, these lines will perform some remarkable tricks. They will gather together in tight bundles in some places, sometimes crowding in so close it would seem they must certainly merge into one, yet they never do. There is always a space between them, no matter how minute. In other places they will fan out suddenly to cover vast territories, all the while taking the utmost care never to blunder into each other or ever once cross one another's paths. I don't know how they manage this, but I deeply admire their skill in pulling it off. In amongst the contour lines, there was a generous smattering of what I took to be elevations, as well as a wide selection of other numbers about which I hadn't a clue. And all this was only the appetizer to this feast of confusions. There were in addition enough mysterious marks and squiggles and colored patches and assorted junk hiding in there that, were it not nearly three feet square, it could have passed for a two-dollar bill from a South American dictatorship. All it lacked for perfection was a portrait of the President-for-Life.

"Looks mostly like a mass of gibberish to me," said I in an unaccountable spasm of candor.

At this Farley O'Toole smiled. I shall not attempt to describe here what that event looked like. I think it may be better to leave it to your imagination. "It ain't that bad, son," he croaked, "you jus' have to know what to look for. Look here," he pointed at a region of the chaos with a gnarled finger. "This big orange patch here belongs to Lunar Consolidated." That was the Company of course. "And right next to it here is where we are." He pointed to a tiny blotch, which I had taken to be the remains of a long-departed insect, but instead had proven to be Lucky Strike. You could even read the name if you squinted hard enough.

"Now pay attention," he continued. "Here's what I wanted to show you. This little green patch here is a claim." He pointed to a tiny square. "An ice mine called the Block O' Plenty. Been there for a couple years and still puttin' out. Now over here is the Hammer 'n' Tongs." This was a little green polygon. "And this one is called the Deirdre or some silly thing. And, see, here's two more." And he pointed yet again. "Now, boys, have a drink a whiskey and look at these for a minute, then tell me what you kin see."

We stared at the little green patches in silence for a minute or two.

"Well?" Farley coaxed.

"They sort of form a circle. Is that what you mean?" said Bemis.

"Good, son. And?"

I stared at the map for another minute and then, very much to my surprise, I saw it. I said, rather too enthusiastically for my own good, "It's a crater, isn't it? A great big old meteor crater, with all those mines you mentioned strung out around the rim."

"Yes," said Calvin, "you can see it's a crater from the contour lines." I hated him for this harmless bit of perspicacity—only for a moment, mind you, but my pain was sincere.

"You got it," Farley cackled. "I knew you boys was pretty savvy when I first saw you." The flattery was as transparent as a glass of beer, but as intoxicating as whiskey, I'm afraid. "Now we'll see if you can put two and two together and integrate. What's wrong with this pi'cher?"

We stared at the map for another minute, then Bemis said, "There's nothing in the middle. There's plenty on the rim, but nobody has a claim in the middle."

"Ha, ha!" Farley crowed. "You nailed 'er again. The claims on this crater are all around the outside of the rim. Nobody's got a claim on the inside. And if the rim is so rich it can support all these mines, then the inside must be rich too, mighty dang rich. There's just gotta be a big comet-head buried right smack in the middle of that crater, or I just turned sixteen and live with my ma."

As much as I hated to admit it, even to someone as broad-minded and forgiving as myself, this story was starting to sound convincing. But then it also seemed to me that it was rather too good to be true. "But say, if you and I and Calvin here can spot this, why hasn't somebody else got to it already?" I asked. By then I knew I wanted it to be true, but was not quite ready to claim such an opinion, since I'd either have to stage a last-minute rebellion or else give in.

Farley said, "They probably could, son, if they had a map. But they ain't. And this here map is up-to-date, too, and that's important. A couple of these claims are new, just a few months old at the most. So you see, they ain't had a chance to spot the pattern yet. And that's assuming they have a map, which they likely don't."

"With all that activity out there, I'm surprised somebody hasn't just come on it by accident," I said.

"Well, there's a bit more to it than that. See, that's a pretty high rim on that crater. Most fellas would just dig into it, instead of thinking to go over it to the inside, where the big payoff is. The high rim keeps 'em out, you see. That's why this map's no good to me. I'm gettin' too old for that kind a work."

He was right about that, from the look of him. And by this point I thought he might just be right about the crater, too. "So why are you so anxious to sell this thing?" I asked.

"Well, like I said, I'm not up to using it myself. And, tell you the truth, there's this poker game about to start up over at the Ice House. I may look like a worthless old goat to you boys, but I know my way around a game of stud better'n most of the men in this town. What it comes down to is, I need a stake and I need it fast. So I'm willing to let 'er go pretty cheap."

"I know I'm going to hate myself for asking, but how much do you want for this map?"

"Hoo-rah!!" said Calvin.

"I need at least three hundred to have a shot at this game, so that's the price. And it's plenty cheap, if I do say so."

"Damn," I said, "I can't believe I'm thinking about crawling up this snout. How do we know this map is on the level? You could have drawn in half of this nonsense yourself. Hell, the whole thing could be a fake for all we know."

"You boys are hard to please, but I guess I'd say the same thing if it was me on the other end." He sat and appeared to think for a second. Finally he said, "I'll tell you what. I'll write down the coordinates of these mines, take them off the map right now. You can send your friend here over to the claims office and he can check them out. It's down at the end of the street. But hurry up and make your move cuz that game starts pretty soon, and I wanna get me a seat afore she fills up."

This sounded like a good idea. I watched him get the numbers off the map, and then Bemis took off for the claims office. While he was gone I went to the bar for another beer. I asked the barkeep if he'd ever heard of Farley O'Toole.

"Sure," he said. "Ugly lookin' geezer, right? Must be ninety years old. He's been around here for years."

"Uh, what's he do for a living?" I asked.

"Hmm. That's hard to say. Odds are he made enough gold prospecting back in the early days, now he can afford to sit in the back of the Eskimo and drink for a living. Sure as hell can't go home," by which the barkeep meant Earth of course." The gravity'd crush him like a bug."

He looked about to move off down the bar, but then stopped himself. "Say," he added, "this O'Toole fella didn't ask you to play cards with him, did he? If I was you I wouldn't try it. I hear he's pretty good, even if he does look like he's about to drop dead."

I gave the man a dollar for his trouble and returned to the back of the Eskimo, brim full of information, the truth of which I never questioned for a moment. When I arrived at Farley's table, I scrutinized the map again and drank my beer. Soon enough, Bemis came hopping in, all out of breath.

He took a large drink of beer and said, "They're all there, Sam, just like he said. I watched the clerk look them up in the ledger myself. He gave me a bit of a queer look about it though. I hope he didn't spot the pattern."

I sighed theatrically again, but knew already that my heart was no longer in it. I said, "So I suppose you're all for this, am I right, Calvin?" I knew full well what the answer would be, but I wanted to have him on the record so I could remind him of it when the scheme blew back and sprayed us in the face.

"You bet," he admitted. At least he was not playing it coy. "This map is just what we needed. We'll be swimmin' in dough before the next sunrise!" That was about two-and-a-half weeks away.

I said, "How about we give you one-fifty, and then a couple thousand if and when we come back with some ice?"

"Not a chance, boys. I'm sure you'll come back with plenty, and you can buy me a drink when you do. But I need three hundred, right now, to buy a seat in that game. Besides, if my theory's right, you're stealing that map for that price, and if you don't believe I'm right then you shouldn't buy the thing."

There seemed little point in trying to bluff a poker sharp. I decided to simply take the deal, by damn, and reserve ample time to abuse myself for it later. In any case, Bemis and I had saved a little over two thousand dollars between us, so it didn't take too big a bite out of our stake. I reached in my pocket and took out my gold.

"You've got yourself a deal, Mr. O'Toole. Devil take me for a fool for making it," I said, and handed over the gold. "Oh, one more thing, though, if you don't mind?" I added.

"Name it, son."

"If you really know your way around those craters, how about showing us on the map the best way to get there?"

"Why it's already marked, son. See that little red line curling up there? Just follow that line. There's a marked trail most of the way, only not once you get to the rim. After that you're on your own."

"Very well, good enough," I said, and we shook hands all around.

"I got to be going now, boys," Farley said. "Good luck and happy diggin'. Next time I see you maybe we'll all be rich." And off he went out the door, moving somewhat faster than I expected given his apparent age.

You may find this hard to credit, given the account I've just described, but the map did prove to be of considerable help to us, especially in the early days of our long journey into the vacuous wastes. The map was the genuine article all right, as produced by the U.S. Selenographic Survey. It was a fine map, especially its contour lines, but sadly, it was not *the* map because it was not singular. As I discovered some time later, when I became a good deal more experienced in these matters, our expedition could have saved itself some money if we had been more deliberate in our shopping—particularly, it pains me to report, in the matter of Bemis's efforts. If he had been just a bit more observant, or a particle less intoxicated perhaps, he might have noticed that the same map, minus a few jots and tittles, was available for purchase at the very claims office he had visited for verification, at the slightly more reasonable price of two dollars and a half.

Chapter Six

Bemis and I had thought we were consumed with "ice fever" before. Now that we had acquired the map we were absolutely on fire with it. I rose the next day so hot with the prospecting fever that my britches burst into flames before I'd got both legs in. I found I could fry a beefsteak with a steady gaze, but couldn't take a drink because raising the glass to my lips caused the beer inside it to boil. Dogs pursued me in the street, thinking I was a fire engine, or perhaps the fire. Wherever I went children screamed, women swooned, and grown men wept.

I confess that some of this is exaggeration. I personally never saw a woman swoon, at least not as a direct result of my efforts, but I did in fact see one man weep. His tears may have been due to an excess of laughter rather than grief, but nevertheless I did observe it.

Now that we knew where we were headed, or thought we did, there was only one item of business left on the calendar, and that was to buy our equipment and supplies. We rose early the next morning in anticipation of it. This time of day, like most others, is determined entirely "by the clock" on the Moon, but by now we were used to that. You'll get little help from Nature in discovering the time of day when you are living underground. When we worked for the Company, we were roused from our slumbers every four hours for the change of shifts by the clattering of a number of electro-mechanical bells. This was tolerable enough once you learned that the din did not actually signal Armageddon, but the first few times were a trial. At Lucky Strike the signs of the break of "day" were more subtle: one had to watch for the drunks to be swept out of the saloons to dry out in the street. And of course outside on the surface it was worse. Generally the only way to tell that twenty-four hours have passed on the surface of the Moon is to measure the length of a shadow cast upon the ground by a large rock or a nearby mountain peak, and then compare that "day"'s measurement with the measurement one imagines should belong to the next. Then, in order to calculate anything resembling a time of day from this information, one must enlist the aid of trigonometry. To discover the day of the week requires the integral calculus, I believe. And even if you can manage such feats of mathematical prestidigitation, you have to measure those shadows very carefully, otherwise a whole week could slip by, right under your nose. That was during the day of course—the fortnight-long Lunar day. At night—when the Sun has gone over the horizon for several weeks of well-deserved rest, and the temperature has fallen to minus a million degrees Celsius, which I'm told is even worse than minus a million degrees of the other kind—there is no way whatsoever to find the time without a reliable clock.

In our high state of exhilaration, Bemis and I scouted the town, looking for the best place to acquire our gear and supplies. Although the lion's share of Lucky Strike was located on the main street, we soon discovered that there were smaller tributaries feeding into it, and at the ends of some of these tributaries we found larger patches of underground real estate that came cheap enough to support the sale of machinery —as opposed to whiskey, which had a monopoly on all of the best locations. We followed these smaller, darker, colder, and even more dog-legged tunnels in search of purveyors of prospecting gear, and after whiling away a few pleasant hours in getting lost, we found one.

The place was called "Dingo Danny's Outback - Prospecting Equipment and Supplies", and it had a large printed, as opposed to hand lettered, sign out front to prove it. We liked the sign, as well as the accompanying hand-lettered banner beneath it that read, "The Finest New and Used Gear This Side of

Alice Springs - Buy It Here Or Buy It Dear - Drop In And Say G'day." Dingo Danny's Outback was located in a large man-made cavern, which itself may have once been home to a mine. We strode beneath the banners and found ourselves in a wonderland of prospecting equipment, some of it familiar, much of it mysterious, and all of it fascinating to us in the extreme. We saw several kinds of steam-powered digging machines and rock drills, as well as powered rock haulers and sleds. There were new and used heavy-duty pressure suits, plus pressurized tents of various sizes and designs, and other items less glamorous but still of great import, such as waste water treatment devices, within which, if the scientists are to be believed, vast armadas of bacteria, algae, and other microscopic beasties fought to transform the unmentionable into a life-giving drink —of water that is. We inspected a small, single purpose Tesla-Faraday resonance engine designed specifically to liberate oxygen from any substance that contained it, even solid rock, or so the sign beside it claimed.

Although the resonance engine, in all its various incarnations, is the indisputable miracle of our age— enabling the human race to do, cheaply and with minimal effort, things unimaginable in the ages prior to its invention—I had never ventured to look inside of one, and could not have told you how these marvels worked for all the oxygen on Earth. I got very well acquainted with them later on, I can assure you —necessity being a very effective and demanding schoolmaster—but at that point in my career, you could have sold me a resonance engine whose insides had been replaced with a butter churn, and I would have been none the wiser.

Dingo Danny had rock pulverizers and ore-testing kits. He had electric stoves and heaters and miner's helmets with electric lamps, batteries to power these, and a device that could persuade a resonance engine to reinvigorate them. And he had foodstuffs, of a sort. There were a number of chickens underfoot in the Outback, plus several dogs, a goat, and even a sow, but few of these turned out to be for sale. Instead he had crate upon crate of vacuum-dried meats, tubers, vegetables, and fruits packed in cloth bundles and sealed with wax. These in theory could be converted into food, or its facsimile, by introducing the remains to some combination of water and heat. Vacuum-dried meat is a Lunar species of that ubiquitous wilderness treat, beef jerky, although in a pinch a jerky of pork, lamb, goat, opossum, or giraffe is also possible. In my experience, the terrestrial variety generally works a good deal of mischief upon the teeth, tongue, taste buds, throat, esophagus, stomach, and especially the bowels, as well as other parts of the body not worth mentioning, and the Lunar variety, created by exposing the meat to the rigors of hard vacuum until a proper rigor mortis has set in— usually about ten seconds—is no better, and quite possibly worse. The procedure is a simple one, and it is just as easy to tell when it has been performed correctly: tap a slice of it gently with a hammer, and if it is ready to eat, it will shatter into a thousand pieces. Box after box of these delicacies were stacked everywhere in the Outback in prodigious teetering piles. (I have to mention here that there is no teetering stack, pile, heap, or hoard in the world to compare with such constructions on the Moon. The patience and forgiveness of its feeble gravity, only a sixth of that found on Earth, makes all the difference.)

As you might imagine, given our present incendiary condition, Bemis and I were ecstatic. We doted upon every new item we encountered in the Outback as if it were a child—our own child, if we'd had any—a child stolen away by Indians and presumed lost forever, only to be rediscovered by us alive and well. We wanted to buy everything Dingo Danny possessed and take a second batch on back-order.

After fifteen minutes or so, during which time the Outback did its work of softening us up for the selling until we resembled two pats of butter left out in the sun, a man came out of an aluminum shack situated at the rear of the cavern. This modest structure presumably served him as an office, and perhaps parlor and bedchamber as well. The fellow had the pallor of the Moon dweller who rarely if ever visits the surface, and he sported an extensive blond mustache. He was attired strangely for the Moon, where nearly every man not employed behind a bar rail or a card table wears long cotton drawers when inside his pressure suit, and a woolen shirt and blue denim overalls the rest of the time. This fellow was dressed in a pair of severely truncated khaki pants, with a khaki shirt to match. The odd, abbreviated trousers might have reached past his knees, but only if they'd made an effort. Atop his head he wore a much abused, gray broad-brimmed hat with a portion of the brim unaccountably pinned to the crown on one side, and, less unconventionally, a huge knife in an alligator-skin scabbard strapped prominently to one bony hip.

Incidentally, there is in my opinion nothing more senseless than owning a hat on the Moon. There is no wind, no rain, no snow, no weather of any kind for a hat to protect you from, and you would need to wear it inside your pressure suit to give it a chance at protecting you from the sun - and then it would press down over your face inside your helmet and thereby bring you to near-instant ruin.

"G'day gentlemen," the man said, and stretched out a paw for shaking, which I did. "G'day t' the bowth a ya. Dingo Danny's moy name an' this 'ere is moy place. What c'n Oi do fer ya, t'day? We 'ave 'eaps a ba'gains, ya c'n count on that."

"Well, we're going out prospecting and we need to get outfitted," I said.

"Splendid! Y've certainly come t' th' roight place. Wot 'r' ya diggin' for?"

I said, "Ice, I expect. Mostly ice. Although we wouldn't turn up our noses at some heavy metals, especially gold and silver, I believe." I smiled in order to expose my worldliness, or Lunacy perhaps, and he laughed politely.

"Good, good! A woise choice Oi'd say, mostly oice. Well now, y'll be needin' a digga then, an' a sled or two fer 'aulin, some tools an' drill bits, an' let's see—d' ya 'ave yer basic gea'? Yer suits, for example, an' yer pressha tent an' yer water reclamation gea' an' all?"

"No, I'm afraid we need everything," I said. "The works." It was starting to penetrate into me how much all that gear we needed was liable to cost. But then, upon further reflection I decided I didn't care. After all, we were going to be rich soon enough.

"Not to worry, mate, Oi've got it all for ya roight 'ere. Let's sta't with the digga, shall we? Can't do nothin' without a digga, can ya?" In fact you could, if you happened to know what you were doing, but that let Bemis and I out immediately.

Dingo Danny led us on a brief but circuitous journey through his vast inventory until, upon circumventing a ramshackle pyramid of fifty-gallon water drums, a huge digging leviathan hove into view. In a moment this wonder was before us, immense and imposing, easily big enough and ferocious enough, if its weapons were any indication, to go fifteen rounds with an African bull elephant and not even work up a sweat. We were impressed immediately, as we were no doubt meant to be. What a magnificent old wreck it was. The first thing you saw, because there was easily an acre of it, was its piebald coating of orange and black paint. The paint was worn and badly scorched in places, but these imperfections only lent it character and added to its charm. A number of fat black hoses came out of the great machine in several locations, then, having seen the sights, dove back through gaps in the hull, where presumably they delivered their goods. In addition to the hoses, there were plenty of intricate and greasy appendages poking out of the great orange body of the digger. We longed to discover the secret of each of these, and how it might be put to work at making us rich.

On top of the whole glorious confection sat a small cabin, somewhat akin to that which a pig driver would call home. We climbed up the side of the great machine, reached the cabin, and pressed our noses against the gritty viewports. The scenery turned out to be well worth the hike, as the interior of the tiny space was crammed with any number of wonderful things: shiny aluminum panels bulged with fat knobs and bristled with switches, each one of them begging to be twisted or toggled repeatedly just to see what mischief it could do. Other surfaces were festooned with clusters of dials or rows of big circular gauges. On the floor near the front grew a thicket of foot pedals, surrounded by an irregular forest of tall crooked levers with big black knobs shining on their ends, and below these a mass of thick cables covered the floor like a nest of snakes. In short, there was enough electro-mechanical mayhem in there to keep a man happy for all of eternity. We returned to the ground in awe. As if all that wasn't enough, the great machine rested on four gigantic tires, each one as tall as a man—and for transacting the actual business, it carried a huge spiked digging claw, curled up before it now in stately repose. Bemis and I weren't about to say so, but we were in love.

"'Ow about this fella now? Ain't 'e a beauty?" He patted the digger's great side fondly. "This 'ere's the top a the loine. The king a the beasts, ya moight say. It 'as its awn self-contained steam plant and a multi-purpose tunable resonance engine; runs on water or grain alcohol or anything with hoydrogen in it. At full throttle he c'n deliver a 'undred an' fifty-seven 'orse power, Oi swea by me mum. 'E's as loively as a 'roo an' as easy t' 'andle as a Koaler bea'. An' the best paht is, Oi c'n let ya 'ave 'im for only twelve hundred dollas. On account a 'im bein' sloightly used an' all."

Bemis and I stood and stared slack-jawed at the King of the Beasts. I tried to tear my eyes away from the Beast, but it was no use—when I did, I immediately began to shake and sweat from the delirium tremens. Could a man really possess such a beautiful thing for a mere twelve hundred dollars? This was well in excess of a year's pay for a picker, but it somehow seemed a bargain to me at the time. But the price was inconsequential. We had to have this fabulous monstrosity if it cost us our last dime, and we both knew it. Dingo Danny looked like he knew it too. But naturally we didn't want to appear too eager.

"Wh—what else have you got?" Bemis stammered. "We should look at some others—don't you think, Sam?" He was trying to put up a strong showing and

I admired him for it, but it would do no good. In the end I knew we would have the Beast or it would have us. No other outcome was possible.

"Well, there's these little ones ova 'ere. Ya moight get by with one a these in a pinch."

He tried to direct our attention to some smaller machines cowering in sight of the King. These other diggers were sad, scrawny things by comparison. We secretly suspected they couldn't even whip a late-model steam buggy in a fair fight. We almost felt sorry for them, having to sit there in the shadow of His Majesty day in and day out.

I tried to stay strong and resist the inevitable, but after a minute of it I was worn out.

"We-ell...," I said a little sadly, "these little things may be all right for amateurs—b-but I suspect we'll need the big fellow there. What do you say, Calvin?" I reckoned I'd leave the final decision up to him. This was more than usually easy for me, because the outcome was in no doubt whatsoever.

"I suspect you're right, as usual, Sam," he said, making an effort to appear just a little reluctant for Dingo Danny's sake.

"A woise choice, gentlemen, 'e's the best there is." Dingo Danny didn't try to hide his joy one bit. He was grinning from ear to ear. At that moment we may have been the three happiest men in Creation, or at least the three happiest men in the Moon. Only one of the three of us had any sound reasoning for his joy, and that man was neither Bemis nor myself. But then I have learned over the years that sound reasoning is something of an impediment in the prospecting profession. It is a way of life rooted in pipe dreams and wild speculations and, if you would like to know the truth, also a great deal of backbreaking work— and the sooner a man acknowledges this, the sooner he can relax and get on with his destruction.

Having declared our intentions, we then felt free to further admire and even to fondle our prize. We walked slowly around the Beast, stopping to engage with each of the King's many wonders in its turn, commenting upon it sagely in the vaguest possible terms, because we generally had no idea what each instrument might do. For good measure we peered into every orifice we could find, where the mysteries were even more profound because we could barely make them out.

"This ah—this part here, its right name has slipped my mind for the moment—do you happen to recall the name, Calvin? No? Well no matter, it will come back to me in a moment—it's in proper working order, is it?" I asked critically.

Dingo Danny stroked his mustache thoughtfully and said, "Ah, that's the steam exhaust poipe, mate, as you no doubt recollects. It works just foine. Every paht on 'im is freshly awver'awled, Oi awter know, Oi did 'er moyself. Don't worry about a thing, he's fully guaranteed."

"Fine," I said. "Just one other thing, though. We might need a few tips here and there on the finer points of operation, never having owned this particular model before."

"Not t' worry, mate, 'e comes with a complete book a instructions. It's up in the cabin. Cabin's fully pressurized a course, in case Oi forgot t' tell ya."

I couldn't speak for Bemis, but I for one was much relieved to find that there were instructions.

"Now you'll be needin' the rest a yer gea'. Come 'ave a look at these suits." He led us away to complete our outfit, but as far as we were concerned the real show was over. We were barely interested.

However, soon we were swept up once again in the pleasures of blind and heedless acquisition, and in less than an hour we had our whole outfit assembled. We purchased two high quality, if slightly used, pressure suits, and a two-man pressure tent, so we could spend the occasional evening indoors and on the outside of those suits. We bought a water treatment unit, plus the water itself, which in addition to drinking also served as fuel for the digger's resonance engine, as it does for most of its cousins on

Earth. There is reason back of the ice fever, in case you were wondering. Ice, or some kinds of ice anyway, is after all simply water in a foul mood. And we picked up a fair amount of foodstuffs, including, I regret to say, a quantity of the vacuum-dried delicacies I have recently discussed (and rightly condemned), but also a selection of fruits, vegetables, and meats put up in aluminum cans. These were expensive, but their contents, unlike the jerky, had kept out of the vacuum and thus had some chance of being edible. We also acquired a collection of tools, some of which, like the pick and shovel, were old friends, and a greater number to which we had not yet had the pleasure of being introduced. We completed this orgy of acquisition with miscellany: a seleno-seismometer, an ore-testing kit, claim markers, explosives, a brace of pistols, and as noted, a pick and a shovel, just in case. All of this wonderful gear was loaded, by us, onto a large sled, with copious advice from Dingo Danny, and secured to the best of our ability with hemp ropes treated with coal tars that theoretically made them able to resist the vacuum and not disintegrate once outside. The sled was then hitched to the digger and we were complete. The bill came to sixteen hundred and eighty-six dollars and thirty-five cents, which, deducting the three hundred already lost to The Map and what we had spent at Lucky Strike, left us with just enough in our pockets for two beers. Not two beers apiece, mind you, but two beers. We had arrived on the field as potentates, and had retired little more than an hour later as paupers, but we were nevertheless content. We were in fact far more than content—we were satiated, sanguine, and significantly satisfied. We were many other things as well, I'm sure, but as they don't begin with an *s* I will have to leave them out.

Dingo Danny, having given our pockets a thorough spring cleaning, was then good enough to show us how to at least start up the digger—and without being too terribly obvious about it, bless his avaricious heart—and we rolled away from the Outback as happy as if we'd been given the keys to the Moon itself. We had the grandest outfit a pair of prospectors could dream of. We had descended on Dingo Danny's Outback, and by the time we'd had our fill, there was nothing left of the carcass but the bones. The situation in our pockets has already been described.

Since we now had everything we needed to start prospecting, excepting of course any knowledge of how the thing was to be done, we decided to abandon Lucky Strike immediately and "hit the trail," as Bemis called it. We had sucked the town dry, by our reckoning, and we were no longer interested in it.

We couldn't decide which of us should have the privilege of being the first to pilot the Beast, so we struck a compromise. Neither of us was willing to "suit up" and ride outside in the vacuum just to give the other fellow more elbow room, so both of us squeezed into the tiny cabin, along with our pressure suits, which together swallowed up more real estate than we did. Thus encumbered, but otherwise as happy as a pair of pups, we left the Outback behind.

As we were still within the official confines of Lucky Strike, and thus not yet properly on our way, Bemis allowed me to pilot the Beast. It was something of an unforgiving business, getting that digger and its accompanying sled through those narrow tunnels, but I like to think I did a fair job of it. I left behind no more than a gallon of the Beast's paint on the walls, and was responsible for the demise of only three advertisements of any note. I regretted those, but not overly, as they were low-slung to begin with. Before long, we were headed out of town along the main street. We thought it only right to give everybody in town the thrill of watching us leave.

Our departure turned out to be great sport for the excursionists, and for the locals as well. They all appeared to enjoy the spectacle of the great digging leviathan rolling along the street towing a mountain of prospecting gear in its wake. Little children squirmed with joy in their mothers' arms, grown men wept, and women swooned. But I recall now that I have presented this same line of goods already, so we shall discount the swooning and the tears. Excursionists stood on the painted aluminum sidewalks pointing and shouting and waving as we went by. The locals pointed and shouted too, but as we were inside the cabin, whose ports naturally did not open, we were unable to hear what they said. They seemed to derive a good deal of pleasure from the sight, however. Prospectors ran into the saloons when they saw us coming and brought out their friends to watch us pass. Some of the men shook their heads in amazement and slapped their knees, while others doubled over with excitement and, resting their whiskey temporarily on the sidewalk, clutched at their sides—and at last overcome with admiration, collapsed to the ground, where in any case their whiskey was closer to hand.

Chapter Seven

Bemis had made an error in judgment during our negotiations over The Map. As part of his campaign on behalf of that overpriced piece of paper, he had let slip his knowledge of contour lines, and thereby betrayed his superior understanding of the ways of maps in general. I'd thought at the time that he had done this in an effort to show me up, though in fact he was simply stumping for The Map, but in any event he paid a price for it, because as a result I was piloting the digger when we left Lucky Strike and he was stuck with navigation. He had argued the point, but in the end he hadn't a leg to stand on, because I possessed a weapon against which he had no defense: namely, my colossal ignorance of the subject. It took only a short time to make my case, and I am proud to say that I was not bluffing. I had come by my lack of comprehension honestly, through years of sloth in general and neglect of contour lines in particular, and when in response to Calvin's request, I had proposed directing the Beast up a sixty degree incline to escape the confines of a crater—a crater that we were not only not resident in, but were in addition not within fifty miles of—he threw in the towel and took over the work. Therefore, when we left Lucky Strike I was at the tiller, staring out the forward facing viewport as if I were peering through the looking glass into wonderland, and Bemis was on the floor.

There were four viewports on the digger: one forward, to which I was attached for the moment, one aft, and one each to port and starboard. These were about two and a half feet in diameter and circular, like the portholes one finds on the lower decks of a steamship, and the glass in them was comfortably thick, plus each was fitted with a grid of steel wire on its outer side to protect the precious glass against any collisions with wayward rocks that might occur in the process of digging.

Although I had proven that I couldn't read a map, at least not to the state of perfection necessary to know where I was, I did know where we were in a general sense—akin to knowing that you are in Arkansas as opposed to Massachusetts—which I hope shores up my reputation slightly. At that time, we were traveling along the eastern "shore" of the Mare Imbrium: a prominent, if largely featureless, feature of the Moon's surface, so immense that it can be seen from Earth with the naked, that is to say the unaided, eye. If you know your Latin, you will understand that Mare Imbrium means Sea of Rains, or even Sea of

Showers, if you want to be extreme. Now, I do not pretend to be an expert on Lunar geography (properly called selenography) or on the planet's meteorology, but I feel quite confident in asserting that this so-called Sea of Rains has never seen a single drop of rain in all of its millions of years of existence. Not one. Ever. It has seen meteors by the thousands, no doubt, and perhaps comets by the score—in fact the scientists say it was created by a single meteor of Brobdingnagian proportions that burst the crust of the young Moon and spilled a deluge of lava across its face. But I repeat (in case you missed it) that this Sea of Rains has never seen so much as an intermittent light drizzle in all its long and tumultuous life. Maybe the eggheads who named it were no more up on their Latin than I am. Or worse, perhaps they imagined they had a sense of humor. In defense of the Mare Imbrium, however, I can at least say that its name is original, not cribbed from some unsuspecting feature of the Earth, like so many of the other prominent items on the Moon. For example, the range of mountains to our east, into which we would soon be venturing in search of riches, is called, if Bemis was to be believed, the Montes Caucasus, and no amount of Latinate whitewash can disguise that theft.

So what I saw through the forward viewport was the flat, empty, gray-brown surface of the Sea of

Rains, with the sky a perfect black bowl above it, and the over-bright Sun blazing away in it like the wrathful, all-seeing eye of God. And stretching away before me, as long and arid as a Sunday school in July and as ruler-straight as the path to perdition, lay the road, reaching undisturbed to the horizon—that peculiar Lunar horizon that is perpetually too close and too sharply defined. I don't know if the road had a name, or whether it deserved one, as, for all of its stark sincerity, it was a decidedly informal affair. It consisted entirely of tire tracks, tractor tread tracks, sled tracks, the occasional forlorn set of boot prints, and absolutely nothing else. No shoulders, no crown, no pavement, and no asphalt. No milestones, no signposts, no advertisements, no fruit stands, and no roadside attractions. No cattle crossings, no pedestrian crossings, no hitchhikers, no broken-down buggies, no idlers, no Indians, and no dogs. No animals, no birds, no bushes, no trees, no shade, no clouds, no wind, no water, and no air. And yet somehow, despite its utter lack of engaging characteristics or interesting features of any kind, it seemed beautiful to me.

While I watched the road, Calvin Bemis sat on what he could find of the cabin's floor. He had set up camp amongst the forest of levers and pedals and cables that rightly occupied the territory, and from there he worked at the job of interrogating The Map. My part was easy by comparison, and while I was theoretically prepared to pity him for his inferior situation, I found that I couldn't, because I was so full up with the satisfaction of mine that I didn't have the room. All I had to do for the time being was to keep the digger pointed along the road—the perfectly straight road—and refrain from dozing off, or dozing too conspicuously anyway. This was in deference to Bemis—I thought he might take it hard if I got too much sleep driving while he was so hard at work.

And he certainly had his hands full with the task. The Map was spread out over his knees, and he peered at it regularly through a large magnifying glass, hoping to catch a glimpse of the faint red line that marked our route. With his other hand, he caressed the digger's Instructions Manual in an attempt to persuade it to reveal the secret to changing the digger's gears, as we were then confined by our ignorance to the lowest one. This marked our first encounter with the Instructions Manual, so I shall take a moment here to introduce that formidable object. The instructions manual was a pamphlet with the same gross tonnage and overall dimensions as a dictionary—an unabridged dictionary that is, or perhaps a good set of encyclopedia. Although sometimes recalcitrant and often incomprehensible, this tome proved in time to be a most valuable member of the expedition, but it was prone to a bad disposition and had the liability of taking up space enough for a coach and four, or so it seemed in the close confines of the digger's cabin.

The instructions manual was an aggressive creature and was not shy about showing its true colors, even on our first day out—although I must admit that in the particular instance I am about to relate, the manual had been provoked. An excess of thinking, or perhaps of dozing, eventually took its toll on my driving, and before I knew it, I had run over a sizable rock—perhaps it was more of a boulder, but no matter—and as a result Bemis lost control of the manual. It danced ponderously about the cabin for a few minutes, enjoying the low gravity, and when it had had enough of that, it decided to land on my foot.

Even under reduced gravity, the pain was severe. I swore an oath as an ante, then said, "Do try to be more careful with that monstrosity, Calvin. I may need that foot someday, when it heals."

"Don't blame the instructions manual. You're the one that tried to mount that boulder."

"It was more in the nature of a rock," I said. "And I thought the Beast weathered it nicely, but the point's taken." What puzzled me about this adventure was that the instructions manual should take out after me, since it was Bemis who was in charge of its interrogation.

After that we traveled on without incident for a while, then presently we passed a train of vehicles going in the opposite direction. This consisted of a tractor pulling six large cars. I let Calvin up off the floor for a moment so he could watch it pass.

"What do you suppose they're hauling?" he said.

"It beats me."

"I'll wager it's ice-rock coming in from the mines," he said eagerly.

Ice-rock was essentially water ore. It contained water and ammonia ices, and other valuable substances, mixed in with the usual moon rock. This was what we were prospecting for. Oh, you could always hope to hit a pocket of pure ice, but that was a rare find. If you did discover a sizable pocket of the unsullied article, you were bound to be rich in a hurry. This was what Bemis and I secretly hoped we would find in the middle of Farley's Crater, as we called it.

"You may be right. Look up ahead, that must be where he's come from," I offered. There was a refinery or mill of some kind about half a mile up the road, coming into view around a headland of rock off the starboard bow.

As we drove past the place, we saw a sign that proclaimed it to be the Rusher Wright Pulverizing Mill and Volatiles Extraction Works. There was a large sort of bulletin board out front of it that gave the current prices in dollars and English pounds for water, ammonia, methane, and other compounds and elements, all listed by their chemical symbols. According to this contraption, which had a mechanism for changing the results by the flipping of numbered cards, like one might find at a racetrack, water was going for fourteen dollars and seventy-three cents a gallon. Then, as we watched, a card turned and the price jumped to fourteen seventy-four! Calvin wanted to stop and see if it would go still higher, but I thought it best to keep moving and said as much. But as we drove on, you can be sure that in our hearts we were urging it on to ever-greater heights.

We passed other installations along that road, most of them concerned with mining in some way, and thus of great interest to us. There was a plant that used huge resonance generators to extract oxygen from moon rock by the ton, and farther on we saw evidence of a farm—but not much evidence. Several pressurized greenhouses crouched low on the surface, but there were no animals visible, because, like the people, they were tucked away underground. We

enjoyed this scenery well enough, but in the end we
decided that the whole area alongside of the road was
too civilized for us. We wanted to get out in the true
Lunar wilderness, where all of the prospecting was
going on. And soon enough we had our chance.

After another five miles or so, we came to a fork in
the road. The main track continued much as before,
bending slightly to the left, and another smaller,
apparently less traveled trail led off to the right
toward the range of hills we had been paralleling
since we'd left town. Bemis scrutinized the map
intently with the glass for a minute or so, then
declared proudly that the red line followed the track
leading into the mountains. Prospecting country at
last!

Our progress slowed somewhat as we climbed
into the hills. The trail wound back and forth more
and more often, as the road encountered more
substantial craters and chasms it must avoid. It was
fairly "late in the day" in the Moon's monthly cycle,
perhaps thirty hours until sunset, and when we went
behind a hill or a crag the road became very hard to
see, due to the contrast with the bright areas still in
sunlight. However, the view was spectacular. The low
Sun threw every spire and crevice on the mountains
into stark relief, and immense pitch-black shadows
stretched for miles across the empty valley floors.

And when we drove into the shadows, stars were suddenly visible by the millions.

"Calvin," I said, breaking the spell. "Do you think you can find the switch for the exterior lights? It's awfully hard to see in these shadows."

He had given up on navigation for the moment and perched on a dormant bank of controls, staring out the ports at the splendid scenery.

"Oh, I think so," he said. "Let me check the manual." In some ways—if mostly inconsequential ones—Bemis is braver than I. He took on the manual straight away, whereas if the task had been left to me, I would have toggled every switch in the cabin before I tangled with that book. Once, after the manual had spent an hour or two probing me in the ribs working to enlarge its territory, I suggested to Bemis that he would be better off to sit on it. I argued that the scheme had several advantages. First of all, there was a chance that the perspective this provided might induce in the manual some small scrap of humility, as up until then it had been inclined to throw its weight around. In addition, I noted that Bemis would have a much improved view out the ports as a result of the higher elevation. And lastly, I argued that the maneuver might enhance his comprehension of the book's contents, because the substance of it would then be much closer to his brains. He was not amused, but my idle suggestion proved prescient. Although its true vocation lay in baffling us with its voluminous and often cryptic Instructions, in time it served admirably as a table, and when we could cow it sufficiently, as a stool. But in those early days, our relationship with the instructions manual was nearly always a stormy one, prone to misunderstandings and recriminations on both sides. The singular triumphs described above were to come later, after much negotiation, pleading, and frequent threats to throw the manual out of the airlock—assuming it would fit.

Bemis started flipping through the manual's pages, and after only a brief spate of oaths, he put it down and reached across me to a row of switches. "These here ought to do it, if I'm reading 'er right." He flipped three switches in the middle of a bank of perhaps a thousand such, and the road ahead and to either side was suddenly revealed in the bright light of three large electric-powered incandescent lamps. I have seen quite a few steam buggies and other so-called "automobiles" fitted with one or occasionally even two of these, but there were three of them on the prow of the Beast, and these were of a considerably larger and more robust character besides.

"Well done, Calvin!"

"Simplicity itself," he declared proudly. Thus Bemis had got one over on the manual in the early going.

Now that I could see properly when we drove into the shadows, I was able to relax and enjoy the view. The digger climbed higher and higher into the mountains, and our spirits soared with it. We had been content before—more than content—but now we were almost giddy with the thrill of it. At some point Calvin broke out his concertina, which may in fact have been his only possession outside of a wool shirt and denim overalls, a pressure suit of course, and a half interest in a large lot of prospecting gear he didn't know how to use. He had adopted this curious creature long ago, and was able to squeeze from its vitals a passable rendition of "Sweet Molly Malone" and even a "My Darlin' Clementine" that could be clearly recognized, provided you didn't listen too closely and weren't too particular about his choice of notes. We sang and laughed and gazed out the viewports at the stars and the jagged peaks and the desolate valleys crossed with innumerable shadows and felt as fine as frog's hair. This was why we had come to the Moon. Hell, I thought, this was why human beings had come to the Moon. We felt like heirs to a spirit and a tradition that stretched back for ten thousand years, to the first flea-bitten cave dweller who decided to take a chance on seeing what might be on the other side of the hill. And we were, too... right down to the fleas.

Chapter Eight

The Beast crawled slowly and steadily up the trail
for hours, so many hours that I grew restless and
consented to let Calvin pilot the digger for a spell.
Now that we had left the Mare Imbrium behind and
were winding our way up the sides of a selection of
mountains—rough, precipitous, entirely fresh and un-
eroded mountains thanks to the complete absence of
weather on the Moon—the job of piloting the digger
was no longer as easy as it had been. The present
terrain made loafing at the tiller difficult, and a
satisfying doze downright impossible, so that what
had once been an enjoyable enterprise soon came to
resemble work. Therefore Bemis took over the
driving, and I took on a new task which I'd invented
for the occasion: short-range or, as I fancied it, micro-
navigation. This consisted of pointing out interesting
features in the surrounding terrain that were too far
away from our direction of travel for Bemis to
observe, and of sounding the alarm when the Beast
was about to encounter a boulder or a deep crease in
the road. I usually managed to give the alarm at about
the time the digger lurched over an obstruction,

because naturally that jarred me awake, but after a score or so of such near-misses I began to feel some slight embarrassment at my tardiness and resolved that going forward I would try to anticipate. After snoozing through a particularly savage piece of outcropping, and being tossed onto the floor as my reward, I took up the task in earnest, and thereafter peppered Bemis with enough nudging, cries of alarm, and epileptic fits of pointing out of the windows to last him a lifetime. Eventually he spoke up and said that, considering the enormous number of alerts I was generating, I must certainly be exhausted, and he insisted I retire from the warnings business entirely and have a nap. As this had been the notion at the back of my mind all along, I felt satisfied and did as he suggested.

I slept for a while, then at some point Bemis called to me and I awoke. I looked out of the forward port and saw only a quotidian slice of road illuminated ahead. But after a moment we came over a small rise, went around a bend, and found ourselves on a small plateau partially bathed in sunlight. The part of the plateau still in the sun was about a hundred yards across, relatively flat and free of boulders, and had an uncountable number of tire tracks criss-crossing throughout its length. It had clearly been bulldozed into this condition for some purpose, although I couldn't imagine what that purpose might be. The perimeter of the flattened area was decorated with twisted scraps of aluminum, a few large, cracked six-foot diameter rings of moon-crete that resembled sections of drainage pipe on Earth, and a sizable collection of spent, dilapidated tires. I tried to remember if we had brought along a spare tire or two for the Beast, but knew immediately that we hadn't. Even one would have taken up most of the space on the supplies sled.

We decided to stop on this small plateau and have a rest. Calvin halted the digger while I did the resting. We were near the edge of the plateau and the view was magnificent. Perhaps a mile or two ahead and somewhat below us, we could see an immense crater —easily a mile across, with steep jagged sides and a broad flat bowl in the center. The low angle of the sun made the ring wall of the crater appear fabulously craggy, and the spiky crenellated shadow of the rim reached more than halfway across the smooth interior bowl.

"That must be Farley's Crater," Calvin said.

"I suspect you're right. It certainly is something, isn't it?"

"How long do you think it'll take us to get there?"

"Several hours at least, I should think." This was a wild miscalculation of course. "The terrain looks pretty rough from here on. Since somebody was nice enough to put up this lovely campground for us, perhaps we should stop here and make a night of it. There may not be a place this convenient for quite a ways."

"Good idea," Bemis said. "My legs are going to sleep on me in any case. I wish they'd built this cabin for two."

Between Bemis, the instructions manual, and myself, we managed to shut down the digger's power plant in a way that would allow us to re-fire the engine and get up steam without a lot of delay. We needed a break from driving, and longed to escape even temporarily from that matchbox-sized cabin, but neither of us contemplated an extended stay. We had feasted our eyes on Farley's Crater, and we were anxious to reach it as soon as possible.

To venture outside meant first donning our pressure suits. This was normally an easy task, one that we could do almost without thinking. After all, we had each of us spent most of a year in the picking business, and thus were quite at home inside a pressure suit. We were in some ways—oh very well, in any number of ways the worst pair of greenhorns in Creation, and moreover we radiated such a rich emerald penumbra of ignorance that we ourselves didn't notice it. But when it came to being out on the surface of the Moon within the cozy confines of a pressure suit, we were as close as you are likely to come to professionals. Anyone contemplating the picker's life should take careful note: you will soon find yourself to be an expert in the care, feeding, and arduous use of your pressure suit, or you will even sooner find yourself dead—fetched up at the Pearly Gates, or wherever it is that you have your reservation—with your helmet ajar and the blood boiling out of your ears as if you were a fountain.

We dropped our overalls and reached for our suits, which barely required either of us to stretch out an arm, since the suits were pretty near to sitting in our laps as it was. I began inserting myself into mine —without much thinking about it, as I've said—but the new suit seemed to be confused as to the particulars of the operation, and soon I even heard from Bemis about it.

"Sam, you've got your leg stuck into my suit."

"I don't think so, Calvin," I said. "If there are any limbs in your suit, I'm sure they belong to you. In fact I'm morally certain of it."

"But no. Don't you see, Sam, that's my suit in front of you, not yours."

"Which one in front of me?"

"The one you have your leg into."

"If my leg is in it, then it stands to reason that it's my suit, does it not?" I said, sealing the argument with, "Possession is nine tenths of the law, you know."

"But, as you will see if you look above you, I have possession of the other leg."

"Hmm." My certainty was shaken by this, but not destroyed as yet. "If that leg belongs to you, Calvin, then please be so good as to move it so I can tell which suit it's in."

"It's in my suit, Sam, I assure you," he said, but then he complied with my request, or so I assumed, because the accordion-fold knee joint of one of the suits—perhaps it was the one in dispute, perhaps not, but in any case the one six inches in front of my face— jerked forward and struck me squarely on the nose. And judging by the force and solidity with which the blow was delivered, it was bound to contain a leg or a limb of some sort, and the chances were at least even that it was not one of mine. In any case, the blow was evidence enough for me, and I relinquished possession of the suit, in theory anyhow. The practice of it was far less certain.

Bemis, the two pressure suits, and I, wrestled on a while longer, until eventually I lost track of all of my limbs and couldn't have told you whose suit they were in on a bet. In retrospect this was not a particularly valuable experience, as such, but if I ever have the opportunity to teach Siamese twins the finer points of ballroom dancing, I feel I could do it now with complete conviction.

Finally I said, "It doesn't appear that this is going to work, Cal."

"Fair enough," he replied. "What do you suggest we do as an alternative?"

I considered the problem while taking inventory of my parts. "I think the only way it can work is for one of us to squeeze into the airlock with as much of his suit as will fit in there with him, while the other one suits up." The airlock on the digger was a container like a Dutch oven turned on its side, but with hinged lids on both its top and bottom ends, and of pretty much the same proportions as the one in your mother's kitchen, unless she has a big one. "Then," I continued, "the one with his suit on can change places and use the airlock to go outside, and the other one can put on his suit in relative comfort and follow at his leisure." And in the end that is what we did, but not before tossing a silver dollar to see who should get to go outside first. It was our last dollar, by the way, and therefore the toss was mighty symbolic, although I can't think of what at the moment. I won, appropriately enough, since it was my brainstorm that solved the problem.

It is an entertainment to toss a coin in feeble Lunar gravity, but don't start this show unless you have most of the afternoon free, else you are likely to miss the third act. The first opens with drama, as the dollar leaves its launchpad in haste and shoots up to a prodigious height, because no matter how many times you try this on the Moon, you will always send it aloft with too much force. The second act is more leisurely, like a long ocean voyage. The coin slows in its rise, and slows, and slows, and then seems to stop dead still in the air, although it continues to spin while in place, as it would on Earth. If you are one of those theatre-goers who likes to take a smoke or a libation somewhere in the middle of the performance —I know I do—then this is the time to do it, as the dollar is likely to linger at the top of its trajectory for upwards of an hour, or so it seems to those who are used to the fleeting one-act performances available on Earth. Then begins the third act, the ponderous, creeping trip back down, which can take upwards of a week if you do not, as I did then, snatch the coin out of its languid, lugubrious, lackadaisical descent and smack it onto the back of your hand before everyone present falls asleep waiting for the final curtain, or starves to death if you tossed the coin while standing up.

So Calvin huddled in the airlock, which I've japed was the size of a Dutch oven, but was in reality the size of a small closet, or a large humidor if you'd prefer, with his suit pulled in after him, and I got myself dressed. Then I checked my cylinders of air, sealed my helmet, and stuffed myself into the humidor in place of Bemis. I opened the outer hatch, and along with a puff of wasted air, popped out the other side and jumped down to the ground, falling as slowly as the silver dollar. Bemis followed a few minutes later, and it was done.

We needed to unload certain items of gear and set up our pressure tent, but I wanted to explore some first. Calvin walked to the edge of the plateau and stared again at Farley's Crater, while I poked around in the discarded materials surrounding the camp.

"Sam!" Bemis radioed excitedly, "I think I can make out one of the mines on the rim. There's a lot of equipment sitting outside of a big hole in the rim wall, and there's a huge pile of rocks off to one side. I think they're loading a shipment of ore at this very moment."

This sounded more interesting than kicking at the selection of defunct tires, so I cut short my inspection of the garbage dump and came over to have a look.

"It certainly looks like they're up to something," I agreed. I think I was a little worried that there wouldn't be any ice left for us.

"If they can pull that much ice out of the rim, imagine how big our haul will be taking it out of the middle." Bemis had found the right way of thinking: this was only more evidence of how rich we were going to be.

After a few more minutes of gaping at the crater, we walked back to the digger to start setting up camp. We hadn't planned too well when we loaded the sled in the first place, so we had to unship about half of our gear to get to the tent. Once we found it, we reloaded most of what we had just unloaded, and set about looking for the smoothest place we could find to put up the tent.

I unfolded the tent and spread it out on the ground. The tent was made of more or less the same material as our pressure suits: a dense multi-layered weave of canvas impregnated with an obscure but effective extract of petroleum or coal tar or something of that sort that served to make the canvas airtight and strong, if a bit stiff. Unlike its cousins back on Earth, this tent had no supporting struts or poles, or ropes, or stakes to secure it to the ground. These were not absent through an oversight, or even out of stinginess or neglect on the part of Dingo Danny, but because they were not needed. It wasn't necessary to secure the structure against the predations of the elements because there aren't any, and the tent itself is held up by the air inside it, once you have contrived to get it in. I put Bemis in charge of hooking up the connecting hose and the cylinder of compressed air we'd fetched to fill the tent. Once the entry port in its side was sealed and the compressed air applied, the tent expanded nicely. When fully engorged with its cargo of life-giving gases, it looked very much like half of a honeydew melon resting face-down on the Lunar surface—a larger than average melon to be sure, but as it turned out, not as large as we might have liked. I was pleased with our progress to this point, but Calvin soon spotted a flaw in our procedure.

He said, "Uh, Sam, no doubt you'll laugh at me for missing the obvious, but how, precisely, do we get inside?"

Being in a fine mood, I determined to let him off lightly and indulged in only one small chuckle at his expense. "Why, Calvin, can't you see? The sally port is right there in front of—" Practical thoughts were finally stirring to life inside my skull, but they had awakened too late for me to redeem myself. "I believe I see now what you're driving at." I struggled to explain the predicament. "As I see it, the air is inside there, but we're out here. If we try to go inside where the air is, the air will come out here, where it's of no use to anyone, and we'll be stuck inside by ourselves, without any of what we came for in the first place. Does that cover the territory?"

"That's about the size of it," he said.

We pondered the situation in silence for a moment, then I said, "I think we're going to have to accept the fact that the air in there right now is a goner." I had picked up this expression somewhere and was eager to put it down if I could.

"A dead loss, I'm afraid," Bemis agreed.

I thought to myself, you can't put the genie back in the bottle, nor stuff Pandora's chaos back into its box. And you can't get the air back inside a pressure canister once it has been let out—not without a compressor pump, electricity to run it, and several hours to waste in doing it. We could refill a canister of air in the digger with no problems—and a good thing too, because we would otherwise soon be out of compressed air to breathe when we went outside— but there was nothing we could do about it while out there.

"We'll just have to write it off and go on," I said bravely. "The question then becomes, how do we keep from losing any more?"

"And get ourselves into the tent with it," Bemis added.

"Exactly," I agreed.

Further pondering ensued.

"How about— " he began.

"Yes?" I prompted.

"We agree the present volume of air is lost?"

"Certainly."

"Then we unseal the door," he began.

"The air rushes out—" I continued.

"The air rushes out," he repeated.

"And the tent collapses," I added.

"The tent collapses, admittedly," Bemis went on, "but not before one of us dashes inside and holds up the roof. Meanwhile, the other man opens the valve on the air cylinder, jumps inside, and seals the door as quickly as he can, before too much air is lost."

"Surely this can't be the way it's meant to work," I wondered aloud. "Besides, then who is left to close the valve? If we leave it open either the canister will soon expire, or else our bubble will burst, so to speak, and we'll be out a tent as well as all that air."

"Ah, I've caught you this time, Sam," Bemis said. "The cylinder's valve will shut itself off when a pressure of fifteen p.s.i. is achieved, or at least that's what it says on the side of the canister. P.s.i. being pounds per—"

"I know what p.s.i. stands for, Calvin. I may not be quite the wizard you are at these technical matters, but I'm not a complete ignoramus."

"Sorry, I didn't mean to act the nob."

"Forget it," I said magnanimously. Bemis is a fine fellow, but sometimes he needs to be humbled a bit.

In the end we adopted his plan of attack. It worked rather well, considering the patent absurdity of it. We didn't sacrifice a great deal more air, I don't believe, and the tent inflated itself to fifteen pounds-per-square-inch in just a few minutes.

Once we had our helmets off, I said, "Good enough, Calvin, your improvisation saved the day. But I still can't believe that's the way it's meant to be done. It's just too bitter a pill for me to swallow."

He said, "The procedure does seem a bit haphazard, I'll admit."

Eventually we had the idea of bringing the air cylinder inside with us and releasing its contents from there, but not that day. I'm told that inflating such a tent from the outside has certain advantages, but it requires the presence of a third party out in the vacuum who is then destined to remain there, and neither Bemis nor I was eager to volunteer for the position.

Since we had been in such a hurry to get inside the tent before it jettisoned all of our air, we hadn't had time to lay in much in the way of provisions. Fortunately, Calvin had pitched in a few aluminum cans and a handful of vacuum jerky just before he crawled in and sealed the door, else we would have missed dinner entirely. Once established on the built-in insulating cushion that covered the floor, we eagerly examined our catch. We realized as we did this that we were ravenously hungry. The weak greenish-white glow that penetrated the tent didn't provide much light—Bemis had forgotten to toss in the electric lantern we'd unloaded—but there was just enough illumination to read the labels on the cans, of which there were three.

I squinted at a can in the dim light. "This one thinks it is some sort of potted meat," I said.

And Bemis added, reading another label, "This one claims it contains mashed potatoes, believe it or not, surrounded by something called 'country gravy.'"

"That could be edible," I said, "depending on the country. It's a bit bent where I sat on it, I'm afraid, but that shouldn't harm the taste any. You did a fine job of selecting the menu, Cal, especially considering you were in something of a hurry at the time."

"Thank you, Sam. I do what I can," he said, then added, "May I trouble you for the can opener?"

"Umm, you must be sitting on it," I tried.

"No," Bemis replied slowly, "I don't think so. So what you are saying then is that you don't have it."

"Why should I have it?" I began, then saw the futility of that approach. "And you are saying you don't have it either, is that correct?"

The vacuum-dried jerky was as abominable as I have previously described it to be, but hunger is the best of sauces they say, and we each had a healthy ladle-full of this to help us get it down—but it was abominable nevertheless.

"This jerky seems a bit off," said Calvin. "Is it possible that it has 'expired,' if you know what I mean?"

"I don't see how you could tell," I replied. "As far as I'm concerned, it expired the day it was created." I looked at the package it had come in. "However, the 'edibility period,' as they unabashedly describe it, still has fourteen years to go. If I'm reading it right."

"Tastes like roast aluminum if you ask me."

"I believe I'd prefer roast aluminum, if you have any," I said.

We ate the jerky, and resolved to put more thought into our meals in future, particularly as regards the can opener.

Not only were we hungry, but we soon discovered that we were exhausted as well. After dinner, we lay back, still in our pressure suits, and quickly fell asleep.

Chapter Nine

I remember having a most distressing dream. In this dream I was climbing Mt. Everest—I have never visited that wonder, but with the airtight logic of such nightmares, I knew it to be so—and I was somehow also wrapped in a shredding canvas sack. It was very dark and bitterly cold, as befits Mt. Everest, I suppose, and I couldn't seem to get enough air, and every time I took a step I sank deeper and deeper into the snow. Then Bemis was there, shouting at me over the wind. His welcome calls sounded impossibly far away.

"Sam!" he yelled, "wake up! We've sprung a leak." That didn't make any sense at all on Mt. Everest.

"What?" I mumbled. "Where are you? I can't see a thing." Then a knee landed in my chest, bringing me fully awake.

"We've sprung a leak," he repeated. "The tent has collapsed. We're losing pressure. You'd best put your helmet on, quickly."

"It's freezing in here," I said as I groped for my helmet.

"Yes. Better turn your suit heater on as well."

I finally fetched up against my helmet in the darkness and got it on. I turned the suit's heater up to maximum. In a moment I could breathe again, and a wonderful, soothing warmth flowed around me. In case you've never worn one, I will tell you that the better pressure suits—especially those destined to be operated in the Lunar night—have insulated electrical wires embedded in their inner lining. When an electric current is applied to them, they soon become warm, then hot, then scorching hot. Soon after that, you will begin to detect the odor of roasting flesh, and at this point you may want to reduce the current—unless you like your meat well done, in which case wait a minute longer. Fortunately, the grilling rarely goes that far, because the battery providing the current soon runs down, and if it is night or you are in the shade, you will be out of the frying pan in a few minutes and back into the freezer.

"Let's get out of here," said Bemis over the radio. "I feel like a ham sandwich that's been wrapped up and thrown in an icebox. Can you find the door?"

"I could do with a sandwich myself," I said. "I'll have a look, or rather a grope." I began feeling around, as I'd done when searching for my helmet, and somehow I found the door seals.

When I released the seals, the remaining air got out in a hurry and the tent pulled in around us even tighter than before. I gradually peeled the tent off of myself, being careful to end up on the outside of it. Then I reached in and helped Bemis to crawl out. It was dark outside, almost as dark as it had been inside the tent. The only illumination came from millions of stars and the half-phase Earth hanging partway up the sky.

Calvin said, "Wait until I get my hands on that Dingo Danny character. He sold us a bum tent."

"True enough," I said. "At any rate the suits don't leak, as yet."

"As yet," echoed Bemis with a sigh.

"We might have died in there, in our sleep," I said. The thought of dying in such an ignominious manner made my skin go cold all over.

"Yes, there is that, isn't there?" Calvin said quietly.

We stood in silence for a while then, contemplating our narrow escape. The blue-green Earth floating in the blackness above Bemis's helmet seemed a very long distance away indeed.

"I don't know about you, but I can't wait to see the expression on that Aussie criminal's face when I pack this worthless tent up his khaki arse," Calvin fumed.

"I'll hold him down while you do it," I said. "But, Cal, there's caveat emptor and all, you know."

"Yes, I suppose you have a point there," he admitted.

We had been far from discriminating with regard to our purchases. In our mad rush to clean out the store, we would have bought Dingo Danny's little old grandmother, sight unseen, and been glad to get her, too. We had been rather stupid, all in all, and stupidity is often a capital offense on the Moon.

"Do you think we should patch the leak now?"

Bemis said, "The only way to find leaks in the tent would be to fill it up again—which means yet more air gone down the drain. I think the smart thing to do is to patch it from the inside next time we make camp. It'll be easier to find the holes from the inside, and we'll waste less air."

Bemis was probably right, but as it happened the procedure he outlined for discovering leaks in the tent was unnecessary, because in reality the tent was intact. And I could leave Bemis's and my reputation intact as well, merely by allowing the canard we'd flung against Dingo Danny to stand—but my conscience would dog me until the end of my days if I did, so I shall come clean for the sake of the peace and quiet. I'm not certain of exactly when I first realized what had actually happened to the tent, but I seem to recall waking from one of my frequent cat naps with a full understanding of it suddenly clear in my mind. I described my epiphany to Bemis, and we had a good laugh over it, at our own expense. The truth is that the tent had not leaked. It had collapsed due to natural causes, because once the plateau was in shadow, and then in full night, the air inside had got cold very fast, and had thus shrunk in volume—and quite considerably so, as gases in a container suddenly made very cold are wont to do. Thus the tent had shriveled until it more or less resembled a prune, or half of a prune anyway. And we had been unable to breathe properly because we had used up most of the air inside the tent, and replaced it with our own unbreathable exhalations. It was as simple, and as stupid, as that. I had no conception of this when I stumbled from the tent, however, and was still riding with the posse that was out to wring Dingo Danny's neck.

"Aw hell," I said, trying to break the spell, "what do you say we load up the sled and go dig some ice? And we can eat some real food out of a real can as we're driving."

"Delicious." Bemis made lip smacking sounds. "You mean while I'm driving, I assume. It's still your turn to sit on the floor."

So we packed up the sled and hit the trail. As the conditions on the road promised to be even worse from there on in, I agreed to let Calvin pilot the digger.

The going was rather slow at that point because it was so dark. And the scenery was—well, the scenery was nowhere to be seen. As far as we could tell, there was only emptiness beyond the bright sphere of the digger's exterior lights. The only thing we could see outside of the next twenty feet of road before us was the occasional ragged picture of the Earth and stars, torn across the bottom by the jagged silhouette of the Montes Caucasus.

The Earth appears much larger from the Moon than the Moon does from the Earth, naturally, because the home planet is so much bigger to begin with—and in its gibbous phases, one of which it was entering then, it should have been far brighter as well. And I suppose it was, but you could never have proven it by us. It may have been reflecting plenty of sunlight, but little of it seemed to find its way to where we were.

I realize upon reflection that I have said little or nothing so far in this narrative about the Earth, so I shall take a moment to do so now. I do not bring up the planet to caress it for its role as the sweet home and cozy hearth of the human race, as manifestly as it deserves such praise, but merely in its capacity as a ubiquitous presence in the Lunar firmament. I was not aware of the remarkable fact that I am poised to relate prior to my arrival on the Moon, so it is possible that you are not aware of it either, and will therefore be enriched by the revelation. Or perhaps you are an astronomer (or are well acquainted with one) and the fact in question is obvious to you, but it wasn't to me, so I shall present it here. And it is this: When seen from the surface of the Moon, the Earth never moves from its fixed place in the sky. Not a foot, not an inch, not by an amount as tiny as a banker's heart or as short as an Irishman's temper. You can stand and watch the Earth all through the Lunar day, then all through the long Lunar night and see no change in its position at all. You may stand there and watch until your food is exhausted, your water runs out, and your air cylinders are sucked dry, or until a hundred such are consumed, or a thousand. You may set your children to work on the project to carry on after you're gone—should you take a break from the work long enough to have any—and your grandchildren too. You may continue the endeavor unto many generations, like the begats in the Bible, and neither you nor any of your descendants will ever see the Earth change position by as much as a fraction of an inch. It will revolve about its axis without pause, and change phases like clockwork—it has no objections to these—but it will never surrender the spot it has chosen in the Lunar sky, not in a million years.

I will lay aside this topic soon enough—although perhaps not soon enough for some—but I wish to make the facts of the case abundantly clear. The only way you can make this stubborn orb leave its chosen spot is to do the work yourself. If you walk, say, a hundred miles—in any direction, take your pick—at the conclusion of this journey you may be able to detect some slight change in the Earth's position, assuming you have a good set of calipers handy and something even more firmly fixed in place to measure it against, but that is the best you can do short of traveling completely across the face of the Moon. If you do that, then you will surely notice a difference. You may decide for yourself whether such a journey is worth the effort, to undertake an excursion of perhaps a thousand miles through a landscape that makes the frozen steppes of Siberia seem like a picnic ground, in order to see the Earth move a hand's breadth or two across the sky.

As I'd predicted, the terrain became rougher by the minute. Fortunately, we had thought ahead for once and carefully tied down all our gear, otherwise, like a Hansel and Gretel in pressure suits, we would have left a trail of water bottles, pickaxes, air cylinders, and slabs of vacuum jerky in our wake. These last would have been no loss, I'll concede, but somehow such items never seem to find their way over the side. The trail's intentions were equivocal at best in this region, and frequently devious. It went up and down and up and down, then up, and then down again some more. And when it had tired of that it tried the same trick only going from side to side. And naturally when it got up a full head of steam it did both operations simultaneously. It was like riding a carnival roller-coaster traveling at two miles an hour —not very frightening, but not a great deal of fun either. The road leveled out only occasionally, but when it did, it made up for that by snaking through fields of boulders that blocked the way at nearly every turn. In many places, there were honestly more boulders than there was road. And in a few choice locations, the road quit altogether and left the rocks and boulders to do the whole job by themselves.

We got lost in a minor way once or twice, to get in some practice at it, then, once we'd acquired the knack, we threw ourselves into it with a will, and soon we established a routine. Every few minutes, after traversing a hundred yards or so without seeing any sign of the road, Bemis would give up any pretense of knowing where he was going and appeal to a Higher Authority.

"Any luck with the map, Sam? Can you tell if we're still on the red line?"

This was no more than a thin attempt at gallows humor by that point. The Red Line, indeed. I'd given up on that old fairytale years ago. I was about as likely to catch a glimpse of the Red Line as I was to get a peek at the Fountain of Youth, or to accidentally stick my boot into the Holy Grail. Why, I was closer to discovering an honest congressman, or the cure for the common cold, than I was to discovering the Red Line. Oh, there was a trail corresponding to the Red Line, I suppose, just as I suppose there is a God in Heaven, but, to His credit, the Good Lord puts in more personal appearances.

To fully illustrate how impossible the navigation was in this portion of the journey, and to seal the case for its complete hopelessness, I will tell you that Bemis fought with the Map without success for ten or perhaps as much as fifteen minutes, then, utterly defeated, rather than tearing his adversary into pieces or sending it out the airlock, he turned it over to me.

We did find a trace of the trail now and then. If we hadn't I expect we would still be out there, somewhere, driving in circles, perhaps as much as a mile as the crow flies from Farley's Crater, with no more chance of reaching our goal than the Flying Dutchman. We ran across plenty of rocks, more rocks than there should be in all Creation by my count, and occasionally, when we had given up all hope of finding the trail, a strange sight would swim into the yellowish sea of our lights. A boulder, exactly like all the rest, would appear, but with a smaller boulder on top of it, and a rock the size of your head atop the second, and if we were truly lucky, a baseball-sized rock on top of that. Bemis and I would stare at the pile for a minute until its significance swam to the top of our rock-numbed brains. Then we would shout together, "The trail! Now where the devil did that come from?" And we would be on the right path again for another fifty yards.

As fine a time as we had getting lost, it wasn't the most fun we had on that leg of our journey. No, not by half. Oh, losing oneself in the dark upwards of a thousand times is a nice enough diversion, for a while, but one tires of the same fare after a dozen hours and hungers for a calamity with a little more meat on it. When we found ours we were not disappointed.

We eventually reached the far shore of the Sea of Boulders, and were promptly stuck back onto the roller-coaster. We were well used to that form of entertainment by then, and so found little amusement in it. It didn't help that the trail's dimensions tended to shrink as we proceeded up the next round of hills. Soon it had slimmed down to a scrawny track as narrow as a bluestocking's opinions and as substantial as a free lunch.

Our pace had by then slowed to a crawl. We would creep up the side of a hill with nothing but blackest space on one side of us and a sheer cliff on the other, and then ease cautiously down the back side of the next, with the orientation of cliff and nothingness dizzyingly reversed. To add to the excitement, we knocked a great many rocks into oblivion along the way, and in doing so reduced even further the already meager foundations of the road.

Eventually, inevitably, our worst fear came to pass. We had neither the foresight, the presence of mind, nor the good sense necessary to know it was our worst fear before we saw it, but once it arrived we knew it immediately for what it was. As we drove over the top of yet another hill, we saw a huge vehicle coming along the road, with nowhere to go but directly through us. Bemis throttled back the digger's engine, releasing a huge jet of steam that turned instantly to crystals of ice as it found the vacuum, and we came to a halt just in time for the Beast and the other vehicle to stand nose-to-nose. Bemis and I peered through the dusty viewports and tried to make out the proportions of our adversary. The results of our investigation were not encouraging. The opposing machine was a monster. It appeared to be a great tractor, somewhat larger even than the Beast, with four gargantuan headlamps and even a few running-lights glowing through a quickly-falling cloud of dust.

We continued to stare into the four headlamps, or attempted to stare past them, and soon saw that the tractor pulled a train of ore cars. We decided there were four of these at least, and possibly five. It occurred to me that this could very well be the ore shipment Calvin had seen being loaded when we'd made camp. We had forgotten all about it.

Once our eyes adjusted to the surfeit of light pouring in through the front viewport, we saw not only the six ore carts that made up the train, but something of the man in the opposite cabin. We could tell that he was somewhat agitated, or perhaps apoplectic is the word. The man was flailing his arms like a windmill in a hurricane, and various sorts of unkind gestures erupted repeatedly from each hand. His mouth was working furiously as well, and the message he was carrying was not likely to be a genial one. We couldn't hear a word of it, of course, which I'm sure was just as well. At that time I suspected Calvin Bemis of being a Baptist, and such talk might have done serious damage to his delicate sensibilities. We kept on staring, and before too long we began to see a pattern in the storm of his abuse. One sweeping gesture was repeated over and over, and he appeared to shout the same set of words again and again. Then he stopped making obscene gestures and instead began to point. Eventually we determined that he was pointing at something behind us. We turned and stared out the rear port then, dreading the worst, but there was nothing there, only the road, or what little remained of it.

"He keeps repeating the same thing," I said. "It's something akin to 'Pass that pup through plaster'. Or perhaps 'Blast it up to faster'? It doesn't make any sense."

"Maybe we should try to raise him on the radio."

"Not on your life," I said. "The material he's peddling is liable to melt the antenna. I'm certain we can figure out what he wants if we just keep trying. Looks like 'Black pit up your masters'—still not right, I suspect—or 'Back it up you bastards'." I shook my head in bewilderment and said, "Sorry, Calvin, I'm afraid that's the best I can do."

"Good God, Sam, that's it. He wants us to back up!"

"Back up? Back up to where? There's no way we can—"

Bemis took his eyes from the forward port and trained them on the aft one. "Damn me if he isn't right. There's no other way. We can't get around him, there's no more than a foot of ground to either side of him, and he can't go around us either. There's simply no room. He might survive the passage, but only by pushing us over the edge."

"Into the abyss," I finished.

"And there's not a chance in the world he could back up," Calvin continued, "not with all those cars he's pulling. We don't have any choice, Sam. We have to back 'er up 'til we get to a place where he can get by."

"But that could be miles ," I protested. "We might as well pitch ourselves over the side right now and be done with it."

Chapter Ten

We decided that, in order to back the digger and equipment sled successfully along the road, one of us should go outside and act as a guide. Since Bemis had negotiated the road going forward, he theoretically knew best how to do it in reverse, so I was elected to go outside. (I had considered tossing the silver dollar to decide the proposition, but had determined that we couldn't spare the time.) I topped off my air cylinders, donned my helmet, left the digger, and walked back to the sled, where I excavated an electric lantern to see by, and a shovel to help in getting the sled over the rough parts. As I'd expected, most of the parts were the rough parts.

I scouted ahead—or behind, depending on how you care to look at it—and signaled to Bemis which way to turn. Unfortunately, the sled and the digger were often at odds over which way to go. When Calvin backed to the left, more often than not the sled decided to go to the right, and vice versa. After studying its behavior for a while, I thought I could predict its future actions by this rubric: whichever direction promised to cause the most trouble, that was the way the sled would choose to go. But even the results of that simple maxim turned out to be hard to determine, as the sled was often unsure which it thought the greater mischief, climbing the sheer wall on the one side in order to upend itself, or plunging off the cliff to its destruction on the other. The one place it didn't fancy, and was rarely to be found, was the center of the road.

Finally the sled came across an opportunity for mischief that was too good to miss. After nearly an hour of "progress" we found ourselves backing down into a steep canyon containing a sort of elbow in the road. That is, the trail went down one side, bent in the crook of the canyon, then proceeded immediately up the other side. All of this on the sheer side of a mountain, of course. The irresistible element for the sled was the deep mound of dust nestled in the crook of the elbow. Instead of following—or in reality leading—the digger up the next slope as Bemis negotiated the sharp turn, the sled got the idea it would be more entertaining to bury itself in the dust. By the time it was finished, hardly a trace of it could be seen.

This mishap was enough for the pilot of the ore train, though. We waved frantically at him to come help us dig out the sled, and he waved placidly at us while driving past. Calvin and I had no choice but to man the shovels, if we could find them beneath the dust, and start digging. We briefly considered allowing the digger to live up to its name, but had not yet tried the great scoop mounted on its prow. Plus, to bring that weapon to bear on the problem would have meant turning the Beast around, and we didn't have half enough roadway for that. So in the end we decided discretion was the better part of pitching ourselves and our gear down the side of the mountain, and did the work for ourselves. It was tedious work, but not too difficult, and soon enough we were back to going forward again.

That was the last disaster we could manage on that leg of the journey, however, and after another brief stretch on the roller-coaster we found ourselves at Farley's Crater.

As we drove along, we could just make out the steep wall of the rim off to our left. And suddenly it became easy to keep to the road, because there were plenty of tire tracks to follow. Soon we came upon other signs of habitation. At one point the road forked, and above us to the left we saw a large, crudely lettered sign made from a slab of battered aluminum. It read: "The Hammer 'n' Tongs Mine" and below the name in angry red letters it said: "TRESPASSERS WILL GET SHOT - SO DON'T!" This was enough for us. We decided not to stop and chat.

We continued on around the rim road, and before too long we came to another fork, and another sign. This one read: "Cube-O-Plenty Mine - ABSOLUTELY NO TRESPASSING - THIS MEANS YOU!"

"Mighty friendly folks, these miners, eh Cal?"

"The best," he agreed.

So we kept going. After another quarter of a mile we came to still another sign: "Matterhorn Mine - NO GROUNDHOGS, EARTHWORMS, SQUATTERS, OR OTHER SCUM IS WELCOME." We suspected we belonged in this menagerie somewhere, so we kept on going.

"I suppose stopping to ask directions would be bad manners?"

"The worst," agreed Calvin.

Our next task was to find a place where we could climb over the rim of the crater. And since we decided it would be a good deal more pleasant to do it without getting shot by the owners of the rim mines, we wanted an out-of-the-way spot to do it in. Before too long our hand was forced: the road turned abruptly to the left again, but this time there was no fork and nowhere else to go.

"What do you think, Sam? Should we try it?"

"Maybe they haven't got their welcome sign out just yet, but let's give it a look. All they can do is kill us."

Bemis drove cautiously up the trail. There was no sign on the road, but when we came to the rim we saw evidence of mining. There was a hole dug into the rim wall and a large mound of rock nearby. However, there was no digger or other machinery to be seen.

"It looks abandoned," Bemis said. "I guess this one was a bust."

I offered a suggestion then. "Let's drive along close to the wall and look for a way inside." Bemis agreed to chance it and we proceeded.

The going was doubly rough beyond that point, as the trail had ended at the abandoned mine. There were any number of stray boulders and black fissures to avoid. In anticipation of our going without a trail to guide us, Bemis had talked briefly with the instructions manual and discovered that levers were available on either side of the cabin—the dimensions of the cabin were so severe that both levers could easily be grasped by one man at the same time, if there was no pilot in the way—levers that allowed the headlamps on either side to be redirected. Manipulating the lamp on the port side allowed me to run a beam of light along the rim wall and watch for a pass. After about a half-mile of searching in this manner, I spotted a possibility.

"How about here?" I offered. "It looks lower and a bit smoother than most spots."

Bemis agreed that we should try it. He chose his approach wisely and we were able to get well up on the rim without too much trouble. But then we came around a bend and were confronted with a sheer wall of rock. It didn't look all that high from the bottom, but it was much too steep for the digger to climb. Instead of trying to back down—we'd had our fill of that kind of entertainment—we decided to go outside and reconnoiter the area in the hope that we might discover an alternative. Soon we were crawling up the cliff face by wedging ourselves into cracks in the wall. In the low gravity, conceivably we could have jumped to the top of this modest, if steep, cliff in a single bound, but as green as we were, we still knew better than to try that sort of trick. Leaping about on the Moon like a fairy princess in a Russian ballet is a great temptation, until you've tried it once and found that you have no control over your trajectory whatsoever once you have left the ground. More men have been killed on the Moon attempting such seemingly innocent hijinks than by suffocation, dehydration, gun fights, explosive decompression, and jealous husbands combined.

It was neither a long climb nor a particularly arduous one, and soon we were at the top. From there, we could see the inside of the crater by the faint light of the Earth and stars. The inner side of the rim appeared negotiable the rest of the way, but we needed to get the digger up the cliff and over the edge first, and for a while this had us stumped. But then, after some discussion, we devised a plan. We would use the digger to tear a hole in the wall and build a ramp up to the top. There was only one major impediment to the implementation of this plan, but it was a formidable one. We had to figure out how to operate the Beast's great claw, and to do this, someone would have to do battle with the instructions manual. Bemis was our man for this, as we both knew. I offered to referee the match.

It took roughly half an hour for Calvin to subdue the manual and figure out what he needed to know. But of course, to read up on fly fishing is one thing, and to do it successfully is another. Nevertheless, I have to say that Bemis performed well. I went back outside to detach the sled from the digger and superintend the operation, and also to allow Bemis the luxury of moving his arms during the procedure, and as definitive proof of his prowess I can honestly report that I was not killed. Bemis and the Beast came close to it more than once, but still I survived. And the plan worked. Bemis managed to knock down a good portion of the cliff with the Beast's claw and make a crude ramp out of the rubble by running over it repeatedly with the digger's huge knobby tires. Before long, we were able to bring the digger and the sled over the mound he had created and down into the crater.

All the fuss of digging and building up that ramp depleted the Beast's precious store of water —its necessary fuel as well as ours—but we paid no attention to that triviality. We had reached the inside of Farley's Crater.

Chapter Eleven

Bemis and I stared into the interior of Farley's Crater with a sublime complacence based on nothing but our own ignorance, and concluded that all we had left to do was to drive out into the middle of the crater and pull up our fortune. And so, refusing to pause for even a moment's deliberation, lest the still, small voice of reason should try to intervene with us, we set off immediately into the crater.

The scene before us, illuminated only by the plump gibbous Earth, a smattering of planets, and the ubiquitous stars, was stark, ghostly, and strange. The inside of Farley's Crater was as empty and barren as any place I'd ever seen, and that is saying a good deal when your residence is the Moon. For as far as I could see, there was not a single surface feature of any kind, nothing whatever to mar the interior plain's vast eerie perfection. There were no protuberances, indentations, or cracks in the surface, let alone the jutting spires, ragged outcroppings, and abundant small craters that were part of the landscape pretty much everywhere else. There weren't even any rocks, and this is a class of merchandise that is never out of stock on the Moon. To my mind, the inside of Farley's Crater very much resembled a gigantic, circular, gray-brown billiards table, remorselessly flat, utterly featureless, and profoundly empty, as there were no billiard balls in evidence, nor any sign of chalk or cues —and more's the pity, if they were to put in an appearance, the balls would likely be the size of the Palmer House, and what a grand game of nine ball that would make! There was no sign of a human presence either, whether in the present or the past, for the good and sufficient reason that there was no sign of anything. If nothing else, I thought, Bemis and I would have the place all to ourselves, and we could claim the whole interior of the crater for our own.

As we started across this vacant plain, we amused ourselves by trying to invent a name for our mine. Admittedly, this is akin to choosing the name for a child that has not yet been conceived, let alone born, but we were as afire with anticipation as a pair of newlyweds, I suppose, and thus it seemed perfectly appropriate to us. We started with a straightforward approach, which gave us either the Bemis and Clemens Mine or the Clemens and Bemis Mine. I favored the latter for its quiet dignity and superior ring to the ear, but Calvin disagreed, so we moved on. We debated the relative merits of CalSam Mine and SamCal Inc. to a stalemate. We tried on Picker's Prize and Two Pickers From Earth, but these came off the rack and could have fit almost anyone, and so were in turn discarded. Next we tried the romantic approach. We came up with The Bonanza, The Glory Hole, The High Frontier, The Golden Nugget, The Golden Earring, The Golden Calf, The Promised Land, and The Milk and Honey. These last few had taken an Old Testament turn, and that somehow shunted us onto a mythological track. Apollo, Neptune, Artemis, Zeus, and even Prometheus were auditioned for the role, but were all let go in the end. Sisyphus was eager for the part, but was rejected for obvious reasons. Then, in desperation, we resorted to cleverness. Bemis suggested The Ice House, The Crater Raiders, and On The Rocks. I weighed in with the Ice Box, and the Snowball in Hell. And at this point, thankfully, we gave up. As far as clever names were concerned, we had struck a dry hole. The Dry Hole and Farley's Folly had occurred to me, but I didn't present them, as they were clearly in the wrong spirit.

I have said that the crater was empty, but as it turned out, this was not strictly true. As we proceeded forward, we found that the interior surface was covered with a fine dust. And the further we went, the more of it there seemed to be. After a few hundred yards it was spraying up in great plumes behind us, which then fell back to join the remaining dust with that unnatural alacrity only to be seen on the Moon.

You may think, extrapolating from the tale I've told about the coin toss, that a cloud of dust (raised by, say, the tires of a digging leviathan) would act in a similar fashion and hang in the air for as much as a fortnight, especially as such a cloud is made of particulate material and thus is particularly light, but this is not the case. In fact the opposite is true, and the mistaken phrase "hang in the air" provides the key to the difference—because on the Moon there is no air for the dust to hang around in. The coin, being a weighty object, takes little notice of whether there is air around it or not, and falls in strict accordance with the law of gravity—which, on the Moon, means that it falls slowly, because, as noted repeatedly throughout this chronicle, that law is poorly enforced in these parts. By contrast, the particles of dust, which are normally accustomed to floating in a nice thick broth of air, find no such luxury here. Like a vast flock of minute Dickensian urchins, they have nothing whatever to support them, and thus fall to the ground at the standard rate—which, although low, still appears faster than normal to the Earth-born, because they have never seen a cloud of dust created without its traditional means of support.

I have abused your patience enough over this bit of natural philosophy, I expect, and will now return you to Farley's Crater, and as I do so I will tell you of yet another wonder. The dust put on a show for us, a performance so spectacular and unexpected that it captured our attention entirely, and did so until we were captured by the dust itself. The otherwise quotidian dust, once disturbed and agitated by our passing, sparkled and shimmered with a million, or more likely a billion, or a billion billion, tiny sparks of greenish light. The sled, soon to be lost beneath it, made a constantly changing pattern of glowing currents and swirling eddies of pale light in the dust, and the material flying from the rear of the tires sparkled as if a constant stream of tiny gemstones were being launched into the vacuum.

"That is simply stunning," I said, staring out the aft port at the fireworks show going on behind us. "Quite beautiful, in an eerie, other-worldly way. It seems we've stumbled upon pixie dust, Calvin, pixie dust measured by the ton."

"Quite a show," agreed Calvin.

"I wonder what causes it."

"It is undoubtedly an effect of static electricity, produced for some reason or another by our passing."

Whatever the cause of the entertainment, its effect was unfortunate, because, as I've said, it captured our attention, and thereby captured the Beast.

After a quarter of a mile the dust was up to the axles of the digger's tires and had begun to slow us down—not that we noticed much. After half a mile, it was climbing over the headlamps, and had reduced our forward progress to a crawl. The equipment sled was by then thoroughly engulfed by the dust, and an odd sort of roiling, glowing, flickering wake danced over the surface behind us, and was the only sign that the sled was still in attendance. We were glad to have it, but it was clear by then, from the labored progress of the Beast, that the sled, in addition to providing fireworks, was also acting as a sea-anchor, and greatly impeding our forward motion. The dust was so fine and powdery that nothing would ride on its surface, except fireworks, and watching it flow over and pour from the prow of the digger, I speculated that it had the consistency of a mildly viscous liquid.

Before we quite knew what had happened to us, the digger was sunk into the dust all the way up to the airlock, and had stopped dead in its tracks. We were trapped like a fly in honey. And just to rub salt into the wound, once we'd come to a halt, the fireworks stopped too.

"Well, Calvin" I said, "I suspect this is far enough, don't you think? What do you say we put the mine right here?"

"I reckon this spot is as good as any, all right," he replied coolly. He took the digger out of gear and banked the steam, since the engine was doing us no good at the moment.

Neither of us spoke again for a while. As I've said, we'd shipped quite a load of complacency at our last stop, and as this cargo had now shown itself to be worthless, we had to take a few minutes to pitch it over the side in the privacy of our own thoughts.

Eventually I broke the silence with, "So, Calvin, what is your advice, do we swim for it, or should we try to build an ark?"

"Beats me. It appears we may have miscalculated a bit, doesn't it?"

"I'd say we missed the mark by a couple of decimal places."

It was time for a rational reassessment of our situation, so naturally we set to cursing and recriminations. We gave in to it with a will, and lambasted everything in sight and most of what was not. This technique is a tried and true one which I have employed with success on more than one occasion, but it proved to be of little help in this instance, and we gave it up once we had run through our best material.

We were thoroughly, completely, and comprehensively stuck. With the sled acting as an anchor, the digger wouldn't move either forward or backward as much as a foot. Yet if we detached ourselves from the sled and tried to drive out without it, our equipment and supplies would be lost forever beneath the dust. And we couldn't afford to lose the supplies. It wasn't just a matter of the money we'd sunk into them, it was rather a matter of life and death. At the rate we had been consuming them, we would soon find ourselves fresh out of both air and water, and would need the sled's contents to replenish these vital resources. We had been profligate in our use of these articles, and the water in particular. The Beast's resonance engine split the water neatly into hydrogen and oxygen, which in turn were recombined through ignition, leading to a reliable conflagration somewhere in the Beast's vitals, which in turn boiled more water, and the resulting high pressure steam turned the digger's wheels. Then, with its energy spent, the steam returned to a liquid state and could be sent around the Ferris wheel again. But the system was not a perpetual motion machine, not quite. Water was lost, and sometimes with drama, as when Bemis had released a great gout of steam bringing the digger to a halt in our showdown on the road. We had been careless in our use of this precious commodity—one more precious even than air, in fact, because a resonance engine can relieve water of its oxygen (which is the component of air that performs the important business, the rest being essentially dunnage), and thus having water meant one could contract for air. We had not stopped to consider that we should refuel the digger from the water cans on the sled, because we had not stopped to consider much of anything in our consuming hurry to strike it rich. So by then the digger was quite low on fuel, if its gauges were honest, in addition to being stuck fast in the dust.

We decided to send out a call for help over the radio in the cab. This device was more energetic than the radios in our suits, and thus could project its signals deeper into the aether, but there was still very little chance of anyone's receiving those signals. Radio only works in "line of sight" as I've mentioned before —and the rim of the crater was high enough, and the horizon close enough, that between them these two factors served to isolate us entirely. It was like calling for help from the bottom of a well in the middle of the Sahara desert. The only beings close enough to hear us were the rim miners, sweethearts that they were, and they were all on the outside of the crater in any case. Nevertheless we made the attempt. Bemis estimated our position as best he could from the map, then we set the radio for maximum throwing power and took turns calling out the coordinates, which were cosseted in a desperate and pitiful plea for help. One of us repeated the message into the radio's speaking cone until he was exhausted, then we switched places and the other took up the call until he in turn was near to collapse, at which point the dismal process began again. While the one of us was calling into the radio, the other presumably would busy himself trying to think of some way out of the trap.

After several hours we took a break from haranguing the radio, after Bemis happened upon a gauge that told us that the digger's batteries had by then sunk quite low. We also realized that we had neglected to extinguish the digger's headlamps, and we quickly shut them off. They were doing us no good anyway, because they were buried in the damnable dust. To charge the batteries would require water to refill the Beast's belly, as fresh electrical energy was derived from the actions of the Ferris wheel like everything else. And likewise the replenishment of our air supply, which was also running low. Eventually we agreed that we must retrieve some supplies from the sled, whether we decided to cut it loose or not. To do this, one of us would have to go outside and swim down through the dust to the sled and bring up what he could.

I am ashamed to relate what happened next. I abandoned all the trappings of civilized behavior and committed an act more heinous than any I had considered in my heretofore serene and blameless existence. I volunteered. Honestly, I don't know what came over me, but that is what I did.

I fastened a length of cable that didn't seem to be otherwise occupied to my pressure suit and cycled through the tiny airlock. The sea of dust reached within inches of the bottom of the outer hatch. Bemis suited up and came through after me so he could hold the line and haul me and any swag I might discover up out of the dust.

It was a strange scene outside. There was nothing to be seen for what must have been nearly a mile in any direction but the perfectly flat, motionless sea of dust, surrounded in the far distance by the crenellated wall of the rim. The dust shone a dull silver in the weak light of the Earth. The only object visible on the whole sea was the little cabin of the digger, with one feeble electric light still burning inside. We should have shut that light off in order to preserve the life of our batteries, but we didn't have the heart, or perhaps the stomach, to extinguish that last spark of civilization, and so resolved to keep it alight on the billion-to-one chance that someone somewhere might see it and come to our rescue. We tried scanning the immediate area using the lamps mounted on our helmets, but we saw even less this way due to the destruction of our night vision, so we gave that up. No matter the lighting, there was no sign of the submerged sled at all.

I climbed down the side of the digger and into the dust. The fine powder began to surround me, and as it did, I began to notice that something was wrong. Because of the quantity of air trapped inside my suit, I was in aggregate lighter than the surrounding dust. Thus I floated in it. As long as only about half of my volume was under the surface, I was fine, but when I tried to submerge myself further I invariably lost control and rolled around until I was once again resting on the surface. It was a very frustrating experience. And to make my distress more acute, Bemis was not behaving professionally at all. Every time I bobbed to the surface like a drunken duckling, he let fly a rude, braying guffaw.

Finally he said, "I admit your antics are quite amusing, Sam, but don't you think you should get on with the job? We only have so much air left, you know."

"Calvin Bemis, you have the brains of a cow. I'd love to 'get on with the job,' believe me, but every time I try to get inside this muck, it spits me back out."

"Oh, I see. I'm sorry. I thought you were performing strictly for my amusement. I expect you need more weight. You stay where you are, while I scout around inside for an anchor."

"Fine," I said, "and where in the name of the priest's pajamas do you expect me to go?"

While I bobbed on the surface like a discarded food can, Bemis disappeared inside the airlock. After a few minutes he reappeared carrying the instructions manual. In retrospect I suppose the choice was inevitable. It was the most massive thing we possessed, outside of the digger itself.

"At least we'll get some good use out of the thing," he said.

"And if we're lucky maybe we'll lose it," I added.

Bemis helped me tie this behemoth to my chest with a length of cable, and I was ready to go back into the dust. As expected, the manual was well suited to the job of dead weight, and I sank quite easily beneath the surface.

I have never felt so isolated and alone in all my life. It was absolutely pitch black down there. A mole in his deepest burrow in the dead of night can see a world more than I could. And unlike the Beast, I was not able to generate any fireworks, or at least any that

I could see from inside the dust. My headlamp didn't penetrate a fraction of an inch into it as far as I could tell. And once under the surface, I was cut off from Calvin's radio transmissions as well. The experience was extremely disorienting, not to say terrifying, and I struggled to keep my composure and not give way to panic. I could move about in the dust, or so it seemed to me, but I couldn't be certain because I had nothing to judge my progress by. And the damnable instructions manual clinging to my chest made any movements awkward and slow.

After what seemed a long period of time spent groping about at random, my gloved hand brushed against something solid. Further inspection using both hands convinced me it was one of the digger's tires. Taking my bearings from it, I worked my way in the direction I supposed the sled to be, holding onto the digger as I went, like a mountain climber scaling a cliff on a particularly dark, moonless night. As I groped my way along the Beast's side, crawling past strange invisible cavities and protuberances, it also came to me that this dust bathing was quite a lot of work. Although I had only just started on this subterranean, or sub-Lunar, adventure, I was already panting with exertion and sweating like a plow horse.

Finally I found the edge of the sled. I groped around even more wildly then, exploring the objects within reach with one hand, while I held on to the edge of the sled with the other in order to keep oriented. It turned out to be very hard to tell what anything was. Just when I was sure I had an object pegged with some certainty, an inexplicable construction would crop up on the other end of it, and I would have to go to speculating all over again. Take it from me, mining equipment is not good fodder for blind man's bluff.

I finally selected a candidate for oxygen cylinder and another for water container. These would be my plunder for the first dive. I jerked the cable several times to signal Bemis to reel me in, and suddenly I was being dragged through the dust at what seemed to me to be breakneck speed. Even though I had signaled for the ride, the response took me by surprise, and one of my precious charges slipped out of my grasp and immediately lost itself in the dust. I gripped my remaining prize with both hands and held on tightly.

In a quarter of a minute or so I broke through the surface. The feeble light of the Earth seemed bright after the absolute darkness, and even through the dusty viewport of my helmet the bowl of stars overhead was dazzling. Bemis pulled me the rest of the way to the airlock hatch and helped me climb out of the dust. I was exhausted and drenched in perspiration, but at least I had returned with booty. I handed my plunder to Bemis and lay back against the airlock to catch my breath.

"You've made a fine effort, Sam, but we don't have much use for an ore testing kit at present. Perhaps next trip you could bring up some air?"

"Oh no. Please say it isn't so," I mourned. "Damn it, Cal, I thought for certain that was a water canister." I had dived for gold and come up with straw. I couldn't have been more disappointed if I had left my head in the dust.

"No matter, you can bring up some water on the next dive." He paused. "On second thought, perhaps that should wait 'til the third. We'll need cylinders of air for our suits first. And we mustn't forget the waste-water purifier, that will come in handy, and more water to fuel the digger's engine of course—oh, and then there's the food."

The magnitude of the task ahead of me seemed overwhelming, if not impossible. "Calvin," I said, "what do you say we skip the middleman and set off the explosives. I'm sure I can find those on the first try."

We plundered the contents of the sled for hours, or at least attempted to do so. It was thoroughly exhausting work, and frustrating as well. The objects we rescued were rarely what we had expected them to be.

We inspected our catch and separated out the few useful items from the welter of dross. Between us we had found three partially filled cylinders of air, two of which we had promptly emptied attempting to find more. We found one small canister of water, and several bags of vacuum jerky. So now we wouldn't starve, but only wish we had. Everything else we brought up was useless.

I sat on the digger, the back of my helmet resting against the outer hatch of the airlock, and surveyed the collection of refuse, or valuable mining equipment, depending on your point of view. Bemis sat on the opposite side of the cab, breathing heavily into the radio because of his recent exertions in the dust.

"Why did we buy all this useless junk?" I said.

"They seemed like sound purchases at the time," he said. "I don't recall you proposing to throw anything back."

"That's true," I admitted. "If we'd spent much longer with Dingo Danny, I fear I would have made an offer on his tame kangaroo."

"Hmm. I rather fancied that cockeyed hat of his."

"Thank God you didn't buy it," I said. "There's nothing more useless than a hat on the Moon." You may have heard this somewhere before, but it cannot be said often enough, in my opinion.

Calvin laughed and said, "Unless it's a kangaroo."

We were whistling past the boneyard here, trying to put a brave face on our situation for the sake of morale, but at that moment I was seriously considering pitching all of the rest of the equipment we'd salvaged back into the dust. If nothing else, it would mean more room inside the cabin—a man likes to be able to lie down when he dies. But this rash if satisfying act was conceived in a fit of pique, while the sweat was rolling into my eyes inside a pressure suit overheating from the dust that clogged its heat radiators, and I soon thought better of it. Instead we dragged the whole lot inside, because there was no other place to put it, and I was damned if I would waste yet more air to get it all back onto the sled, assuming that I could find it, or cared to.

I regretted the decision almost immediately. This largely irrelevant collection of supplies completely filled what little space had been left in the cabin for the pilot, let alone passengers. There soon arose a dispute between me, the tent, and the empty air canisters over who would occupy the Dutch oven, and when negotiations failed and the tent refused to fit, I was declared the victor and took up residence. But I must say that I never would have succeeded in this without Bemis. He pointed out that if any of the gear occupied the airlock, we would be obliged to shift it somewhere else every time we wanted to venture outside.

Neither Calvin nor I had been able to locate the water purifier, which would have been a blessing. We had each of us by then accumulated a sizable quantity of impure water, if you get my meaning, which sooner or later we must unship or else explode, and we had no place to stow it but in the original containers, which were by then unpleasantly, not to say painfully, full. The water purifier was the right answer for this, but after twelve miserable excursions into the dust, and two cylinders of air expended in the search, it was nowhere to be found. Still, there is a limit to any man's endurance under such pressures, and in desperation we decanted a few slabs of vacuum jerky from their pouches and replaced them with the impure fluids, the process being punctuated by grateful sighs of relief. (The comparison of the qualities of vacuum jerky to those of a pouch full of warm—fluids—originally slated for this space has been thoughtfully eliminated.) And thus its robust bouquet was added to the already close atmosphere of the cabin, and did not improve it much. Any amount of water was precious by that time, however, and we dared not take it out the airlock and throw it over the side as we had done previously, in the halcyon days of our complacence. Bemis put it succinctly: "We can't afford to piss it away," he insisted.

Despite considerable effort, we had been unable to detach the sled from the digger. As Archimedes surely would have appreciated, there was no way to get any leverage on the thing to pull it loose, so we returned to the cabin and tried once more to move the digger with the sled attached. We built up steam and released the engine at full throttle, but it still would not budge, and finally we were obliged to give it up. After that we sharpened our teeth on bricks of vacuum jerky, then stared out the viewports at the sea of dust, and pondered our fate. Just a few hours ago, we had been certain we were about to be rich. Now we were nearly as certain that we were about to be dead.

Between the two of us, we had enough air to last about forty-eight hours, or twenty-four hours apiece if we both intended to breathe full time. We had tried mightily to create more by enlisting the resonance engine, but as it turned out, the procedure required that the whole Ferris wheel be in operation, or at least the greater part of it, and there was not sufficient water left for much of that—even if it would run when the wheels couldn't move, which we were unable to persuade it to do. So we couldn't drive out, and our chances of being rescued before our air gave out were awfully slim. Realistically, I suppose, they were zero. No one could hear our intermittent and increasingly pathetic pleas for help unless he was inside the crater—and it was thoroughly deserted, and had been for the better part of a billion years.

We couldn't think of anything else to do, so Bemis and I passed the time with another round of cursing and recriminations. This time, we had the benefit of experience, and so set about the task systematically. After all, the orgy of acrimonious character assassination we were about to embark upon would probably be the last thing we would have a chance to do in this life. We wanted ever so badly to do something right before we died, and this employment, unlike prospecting or staying alive past sunrise, seemed within our range. Calvin wanted to dig into his past and haul aboard old schoolmasters and playground bullies for treatment, but I objected to this, despite its admirably thorough intentions, because after all the air was low, and I was anxious to ensure that the prominent villains of the piece not receive superficial work simply because we ran out of air and died.

So we proceeded in chronological order of contribution to our demise. First we assassinated Fat

Boy. Next we flagellated Farley O'Toole. Then we demolished Dingo Danny. We lambasted the entire population of Lucky Strike, both permanent and transient, and did them one by one, making up names and biographies as necessary, and lavished particular attention on prospectors and all excursionists past, present, and future. If you are looking for the part each of these villains played in our destruction, then you are excused, as they are all of them innocent as newborn babes—with the possible exception of Farley O'Toole, who marked his goods up rather steeply for greenhorns—but then the purpose of the exercise was not in seeking after truth, but more in the way of its opposite. We gave a fine shellacking to the volatile driver of the huge rig that had blocked our way on the road, and held a special session to roast the owners of the rim mines and their damnable ungrammatical no-trespassing signs. And in case you are sensing a vacuum at the heart of the enterprise, where two featherbrained, no-account ex-pickers should be prominently displayed, you will be pleased to hear that we finally came around to cursing ourselves. For thoroughness's sake we did each of us separately, then took on the pair as a corporation.

Eventually the well of recriminations ran dry—and yet we found that somehow we were still alive. We tried not to be too disappointed. However, we soon came up with a new diversion and started on a round of pointless rhetorical questions. Why had we been so stupid? (This covered a good deal of territory, for a certainty.) Why hadn't we been content to stay pickers? Why had we trusted that crooked old fossil Farley O'Toole and followed his succubus of a map? And how had we allowed ourselves to get stuck in this damnable dust-choked crater? How could we have been so stupid? Why hadn't we been content to stay pickers? . . . and so the rhetorical questions were a bust. At last, in desperation, we gave ourselves over to maudlin sentimentality and started talking about the Good Old Days. We discussed all the grand fellows we had met while working for the Company, even recalling their names, the less repellant aspects of their features, and whatever worthwhile qualities we could remember, the advantage in this sort of operation being that it is often so difficult that it holds one's attention admirably. We fantasized about the happy times back at the Company mess, drinking and lying and humiliating ourselves trying to impress the females thereabouts. Lord, what happy times those were! What carefree times. Why had we ever thought of leaving such a paradise?

This proved to be a most satisfying way to fritter away the remainder of our lives, and after some hours of such talk we fell asleep.

Epilogue

As you may have guessed, or not, Bemis and I didn't die, not there and then anyway. There was in fact quite a lot of adventure, and a world of trouble, still ahead for us. But if you would like to know the particulars, you'll have to read Mark Twain on the Moon Book 2: The Deirdre..

Made in the USA
Middletown, DE
25 April 2019